Royal REBEL

DESIGNER

CARINA AXELSSON

USBORNE

Chapter ONE

3.45 p.m., Monday, in the private garden at the palace

Hi Tiara Girl! And welcome to your channel!

Your most recent video: <u>Tiara Girl's Top Five Tips for Wearing a Tiara</u> has had:

19,997 views

HOLY ROYAL MACARONI!!

I stop in my tracks. I bring my phone close to my eyes. Nearly 20,000 views? And only since late

Friday night? It can't be true!

I refresh my phone's screen.

20,011 views...

OMG! For the first time **EVER**, one of my Tiara Girl vlogs has passed 20,000 views!

I let out a scream of excitement as I sprint across the gardens towards the palace, arms pumping, my hair flying behind me. I drop my rucksack and do three cartwheels in quick succession on the springy grass behind the perfectly clipped topiary bushes. As I whirl along I can make out a few of the palace gardeners, who smile at me as I fly past. I spring back to my feet and am just about to let out another "Yippee!" when my security team reaches my side, breathing hard, panicked looks on their faces. I know what they are going to ask and my excitement fizzles away faster than my pony, Cupcake, can canter.

"Your Royal Highness, is everything all right?"

You see, this is the thing about being a princess... *sometimes it's easy to forget that I am one.* Which means that sometimes it's also easy to forget that wherever I go, my security team goes too.

I mean, I know my family has been ruling the Queendom of Waldenburg for centuries and I'm next in line to be queen, but for me that's…well, *normal*. It's not like I go around thinking, *I'm a future queen and I have to be careful that nothing happens to me* – especially when I have mega-super good news on my mind!

But my security team is **ALWAYS** on high alert, so, if I suddenly scream loudly and take off at a lightning-fast run before disappearing from view behind some bushes, I guess it's their job to freak out.

"Everything is…great," I say while the head of security, Julia, anxiously looks me over from head to toe. I feel my smile start to freeze on my face while I try to come up with a quick excuse for my antics.

If you're wondering why I can't tell Julia the truth, then here's why… Royal Confession: I cannot tell her because *my vlog is secret*. The only other person who knows about it is my **BFF**, Leonie Leonberger – and that's how it has to stay.

I know you must be wondering why I have to keep my vlog a secret – I mean, a princess can do whatever she wants, right?

WRONG.

A princess – especially when she is the heir to a throne – is not supposed to be interested in fashion. It's not *appropriate*, as my grandmother and mum like to remind me. According to the palace, I should be focused on my royal duties so that I will better be able to serve Waldenburg after my official coming of age (aka my fourteenth birthday).

Therefore, vlogging is out – *especially* vlogging about *fashion*.

As Grandmaman puts it: "People will not take you seriously as a queen if they see you are too interested in fashion. You can do one or the other, but not both."

When I told Grandmaman that in that case I'd happily choose a future in fashion, she said, "I'm afraid destiny has singled you out to be a queen, Lily, and we can't change that. You represent nine hundred years of royal Waldenburg tradition – *you* are living history."

Whatever that means!

Finally I tell Julia that I'm just excited to be home from school. Julia looks a bit confused by my answer and I don't blame her, but what else am I supposed to say? But as I'm obviously all right she smiles and says, "It's always a nice feeling to be back home."

"Exactly." I keep smiling.

PHEW!

My cocker spaniel, Coco, suddenly comes rushing across the garden, her tail wagging madly. She hurls herself at me, barking loudly, and Julia disappears into the background. I pick up my rucksack and swing it over my shoulder as Coco and I skip into the palace through a side entrance.

Alice is waiting for me when I walk into the Marble Hall. Alice is Alice Victoria, Countess of Vendelstein, Mistress of the Robes to the Royal Court of Waldenburg and a former general of the Waldenburg army. She works for my mum, organizing her official trips and managing the schedules of her ladies-in-waiting amongst other things – although I often think her main responsibility is keeping tabs on me and making sure I look and act like a princess **AT ALL TIMES**.

Her white helmet of hair is gleaming in the afternoon light and she is holding a thick folder in her hand. She is dressed in a navy skirt and matching jacket, a silk scarf and a pair of court pumps. A discreet brooch in the form of a bumblebee is pinned to the left lapel of her jacket. As I walk in Alice looks me over with her steely blue eyes.

"Why is there grass in your hair, Princess Lilian?"

I catch sight of my reflection in one of the large, elaborately carved mirrors behind her. I have to admit, there is quite a bit of grass stuck to the ends of my brown, shoulder-length hair.

"It's from the cartwheels I did outside. I guess the lawns have just been cut," I answer as I smile and twirl away from her towards the enormous white marble staircase that sweeps up to the ballroom.

Alice follows me, her heels clicking loudly on the floor. "Please make sure it's all brushed out for your Princess Class later this evening. The Queen Mother will be present…"

The Queen Mother is my grandmaman.

"Don't worry, Alice. I'll look like the perfect princess, I promise!"

Alice rolls her eyes. "Speaking of your Princess

Class— If you could please stop twirling for one moment, Princess Lily...thank you. Your studies on Waldenburg politics and history have been postponed; Professor Hustemeier is ill."

"So why isn't class cancelled?"

Alice clears her throat loudly. "Because I will teach today's class instead – and it's an especially *important* and exciting one."

"It is?"

Alice nods. "Yes. Your grandmother has a very nice surprise for you. She'll come by especially to talk to you about it."

I stop and stare at Alice. "What is it? Can you tell me?"

"I'm not at liberty to say. But the Queen Mother is very excited." Alice smiles.

OMG! I'm **SO** thrilled, because even though Alice isn't saying anything, I'm like 99.9999 per cent sure I know what Grandmaman's surprise is: *I think she wants me to design a ballgown!!!* Which is basically my dream, because I love to design dresses and make them, and then vlog about them afterwards. And how cool would it be to do that with a real-life ballgown?

Okay, I admit Grandmaman hasn't exactly *said* that she wants me to design a ballgown...but still... last week, at least twice, she very carefully – and for a *very* long time – studied some ballgown sketches I'd drawn. She also told me she really, really liked them *and* she made a point of saying that *they gave her an idea...*

And, I mean, what other idea could they have given her?

Especially when you consider that I need a ballgown for my birthday ball when I turn fourteen in the spring.

Just thinking about it is so exciting that I start twirling around Alice again. "That's great, Alice, I can't wait!"

"Good. Then I'll see you at 6 p.m." Alice catches my eye and looks sternly at me. "And remember..."

I know what Alice is about to say.

"A princess is never late!" I chant at exactly the same time as her. Then I dash up the stairs, Coco at my heels, before she can mention anything else.

I bet you're wondering why I need Princess Classes when I'm already a princess. Here's why: because I'm the heir to the throne. And ever since our queendom was founded in 1073, every Crown Princess of Waldenburg has officially started her royal duties on her fourteenth birthday – the day she "comes of age" (as Grandmaman and the palace put it). Basically, Princess Class is the palace's way of making sure I'll know exactly how to be the **PERFECT** princess by the time my birthday rolls around and I have to start with my official royal duties.

But before you start thinking, *Wow, how exciting to start royal duties and ride in an open-top carriage and wave at crowds and attend balls and wear tiaras,* let me just point out the following:

THREE THINGS I KNOW WILL HAPPEN WHEN MY OFFICIAL ROYAL DUTIES BEGIN:

1. I will be able to act as regent, which means that

I can act on my mother's behalf if she is out of the country. So, for example, I can sign laws into existence, inspect military troops and sit in on parliamentary sessions. Which, okay, might be important, but I can't say it makes me want to do cartwheels of joy.

2. I will have my monogram (two back-to-back interlacing "L"s, for Lilian, with the royal Waldenburg crown above) embossed on all my personal belongings – including my stationery. Because, according to Alice, "Social media messaging is all fine and dandy, Princess Lily, but people expect a written letter of thanks from a Crown Princess. And you will write even more letters after you become queen. It's a lovely tradition." This is exactly the kind of thing they never mention in fairy tales.

3. I will begin presiding alongside my mother at official events. This means, for instance, that when a head of state visits, I must join my parents and greet her or him at the airport, attend formal banquets and speak

knowledgeably to them about the politics and culture of her or his country. When I told Alice that there is no way I can know about the politics and cultures of all the countries in the world, Alice said not to worry because the palace will always brief me beforehand. I'm not sure whether I'm supposed to be happy about this or not.

Anyway, now you know why I need Princess Class...

As soon as I walk into my bedroom I let my guinea pig Zoë out of her cage (she's royally cute!!!) so she can run around my room while I do my homework. Then I quickly send Leonie a message:

Me: Grandmaman is going to stop by my Princess Class because she has a surprise for me... I bet she's going to ask me to design my ballgown for my birthday. I'm so excited!!!

Leonie: OMG! It's about time she tells you about her idea. She's been hinting at it for long enough! I mean, the way she kept looking at your drawings last week…

Me: I KNOW!!! It will be so awesome if I'm right because I could try some new sewing and customizing techniques. I already have plans for a video: Tiara Girl's Top Ten Tips for Making a Ballgown!

Leonie: Yes!!! And I could help you film it because it would be great to have some close-ups of you sewing sequins on and stuff…

Me: And then I could make Coco a matching ribbon for her neck and Zoë a matching tutu!

Leonie: That would be SO ADORABLE!

YAY! This is why Leonie and me are besties: we totally think like twins!

I say goodbye so I can quickly finish my homework, then change into a pair of riding breeches and a fleece jacket before Coco and I leave for the stables.

When I arrive, the Head Groom is waiting to help me but I like to do as much as I can for Cupcake myself, so after I've groomed and saddled her,  I mount her and together with Coco we head to the private part of the palace park.

Once we reach my favourite hidden valley I let the reins slip through my fingers and Cupcake immediately shoots off like an arrow. I can't help but smile as I lean forward and flatten myself along her back – I feel as if I'm leaving the world behind: the palace, Alice, school, homework – everything! I love the way Cupcake snorts with happiness as we canter on and I'm sure she enjoys the freedom as much as I do. Her thick blonde mane blowing in the wind tickles my face and by the time we slow down my eyes are watering from the long gallop.

As we walk back to the palace, giving Cupcake a chance to cool down, I realize that I haven't included her in a video since I made my second vlog: Get Your Pony Glitzed Out – Tiara Girl Style. I think it's time for another pony special...

Back at the stables, I unsaddle Cupcake, rub her down with a brush and rag, clean her hooves and lead her into her stall. I quickly give her a goodbye kiss on her velvety nose and feed her a carrot, then I race back to my room, Coco at my heels. I change into a pair of jeans I've customized with colourful patches, a white ruffle blouse and my favourite **DIY** rhinestone bracelet. (I glued some rhinestones onto a leather band and then made a button fastening for it. **LOVE!**)

Before I leave my bedroom I make sure to put all my favourite ballgown sketches together in one of the portfolios I use to hold my drawings – just in case Grandmaman wants to see them again.

 # Chapter TWO

6 p.m., Princess Class in Grandmaman's sitting room

Alice is on the phone as I walk into Grandmaman's powder-blue sitting room. She waves at me and holds one finger up, meaning that she'll only be a minute. I head straight to the sofa facing the fireplace and sink into the plump blue silk cushions. As I open my portfolio and arrange my sketches, Coco curls up beside me and looks at me with her huge cocker spaniel eyes. I kiss her on her topknot because she is so gorgeous!

Alice finishes her call and then sits in the armchair to my left. I wait while she shuffles through the papers in the enormous binder she's holding. Finally she stops and peers at me intensely. "I have some very exciting news for you…"

I can hardly sit still.

"Because your fourteenth birthday is fast approaching…"

"I know, Alice, I know! That's why I've brought these ballgown drawings with me – I'm sure one of them could be perfect for my birthday ball. I especially like this glittery yellow one…"

But Alice isn't looking at my sketches.

"Yes, lovely… However, Princess Lily, as I was saying, I have some very exciting news for you."

Huh? If Alice isn't going to talk about my birthday ballgown, then what *is* her exciting news…?

"This Friday morning you will attend a ribbon-cutting ceremony and royal walkabout."

"Okay…will I be with my mum? Or Dad? Or Grandmaman?"

Alice smiles. "In the past you have always accompanied your parents and grandmother to these kind of events – but here's the exciting news: this time, you will be *on your own…"*

My eyes widen till I'm sure my eyeballs look like golf balls.

On my own?

"We – your parents, the palace and myself – feel it is time," Alice continues. "Everyone is delighted for you."

I sit, frozen on the sofa, while Alice continues to smile at me.

Finally I manage, "But I don't turn fourteen for another six months! I thought I'd start with official duties after my birthday?"

"Official duties, yes…but before then you must have some real-life solo experience. This is to ensure that you will be confident and at ease in your role as a *working* Crown Princess. There won't be time to practise later – we must begin now."

"But I have no idea what I'm supposed to do!"

"That's the point, Princess Lily – you must learn, and a princess learns best by *doing."* Alice hands me a large white envelope with a sticker that has *HRH*

CROWN PRINCESS LILIAN printed on it, with the royal crown of Waldenburg just above it. "In this envelope you will find all details concerning the event, plus your schedule. There is also a copy of the speech you will give."

"**SPEECH!!!** What speech?!"

"The one you must give before you cut the ribbon."

"But—"

"We can finalize the speech together so that you're pleased with the wording. It's very short, I promise," Alice adds cheerily. "You'll memorize it in no time."

"But—"

"No buts, Lily," Alice interrupts. "You are about to begin a very important new chapter in your life."

I could cry! I don't feel ready for this **AT ALL**!

Alice clears her throat and presses on. "The Hairy Hounds and Happy Horses Animal Rescue Centre has just moved to bigger premises and on Friday morning you will open their new centre. The palace thought that because of your love of animals, this would be a good fit for you. At the end of the ceremony you will be introduced to a foal that was recently brought to the centre and which has been named Lilian in your honour." From her folder Alice pulls out a photograph and hands it to me. "This is Lilian."

Lilian is a very pretty chestnut Waldenburg Mountain Pony. On the back of the photograph it says that her owners had abandoned her in the forest, thinking she would survive on her own. Thank goodness she was taken to the rescue centre.

After a short pause Alice adds, "Once the palace confirms your appearance at the rescue centre, I think we can expect quite a strong turnout to see you. We estimate crowds of a thousand spectators or more."

My mind is whizzing so fast I can't speak. I mean, I've never done a walkabout on my own! With my parents, yes – they've taken me on quite a few. I've followed them as they literally "walk about" and meet the crowds. They shake hands and smile and are friendly with everyone – Mum always has to accept lots of flower posies… But this time the focus will be on me! And how am I supposed to give a speech in front of **A THOUSAND** or more people? **HOW?** And what about the ribbon cutting? What if the scissors slip from my hand just as I'm trying to cut the ribbon? I'll go down in the history books as Lily the Clumsy.

I'M ROYALLY DOOMED!!!

"And don't worry about a thing. I'll be with you every step of the way. It will be fun – you'll see."

FUN?!! The only part that seems remotely fun is meeting Lilian the foal.

I crash back into the sofa and try not to cry.

But suddenly I sit bolt upright. "But, Alice, I'm supposed to be in school on Friday morning. What about Maths and History? What about learning Waldenburgerish verb conjugations?"

"The palace and I have already contacted your school to discuss Friday – and the future."

"The future?"

Alice nods. "From now on your Princess Class will include regular real-life royal duties – solo ones. Therefore the palace and I are liaising with your teachers to find a way to make sure you keep up with your assignments while also fulfilling your increased royal obligations."

WHAT?!!

Alice is smiling as she informs me of some of the other practical lessons she has scheduled: the opening of a new exhibition on nineteenth-century Waldenburg steam trains, cutting the ribbon at the new children's hospital in the village of Lientz, presenting the trophy for the best mountain cheese at this winter's Waldenburg Farmers' Collective Show...and on and on.

I am in shock. I mean, if my new princess schedule is going to be chock-a-block, how am I supposed to find time for Tiara Girl? **HOW?** Will I still be able to film videos? It's hard enough to keep it a secret without having to fit it in between giving speeches at cheese contests and cutting ribbons all over Waldenburg!

I must look as excited as I feel, which is basically about -2,718 on a scale of one to ten because Alice suddenly stops and peers at me over her reading glasses. "I know it is a lot to take in but I and everyone at court will help you with everything – including your wardrobe."

"My wardrobe?"

Alice nods. "Yes, your *working* wardrobe. Your new duties will require some new outfits – but they will have to conform to certain rules. Customized jeans and glittery patchwork are out," Alice says, pointedly glancing at my jeans and shirt. "You must look appropriate – and smart and polished."

"Smart and polished?" I say loudly. I know what this means: safe and boring! So **NOT** my style.

Alice nods and from the depths of her binder she whips out an official-looking paper with my mum's monogram at the top of it. "This is something the palace and I have come up with just for you."

XII

HRH CROWN PRINCESS LILIAN
WARDROBE GUIDE

To ensure that HRH Crown Princess Lilian will be able to fulfil her upcoming royal duties with style, comfort and elegance, Alice Victoria, Countess of Vendelstein, Mistress of the Robes, will oversee HRH Crown Princess Lilian's new wardrobe, using the following guidelines:

1. Fabrics must withstand wrinkling with minimal or no effect, even after long seated ceremonies.

2. Waldenburg wool is to be favoured where possible.

3. Solid colours preferred. Must be easily visible in a crowd or on television.

4. Black is for funerals only.

5. No jeans when on official royal duty – except at a rodeo on a state visit to the United States of America. This is to be discussed in accordance with royal protocol and the Ministry of Foreign Affairs as part of any official preparations for the trip.

6. A new Waldenburg national folk costume is to be custom-made for HRH Crown Princess Lilian, complete with the flouncing on the apron edge that signifies a young woman has come of age.

7. No glitter, sequins or metallic fabrics.

8. No patches or customizing of any kind unless approved by the Countess of Vendelstein.

OMG!!!

A whole new set of rules – Royal Rules! As if this Princess Class could have got any worse!!!!

I mean, look at Rule Number 5: I'm not supposed to wear jeans if I'm doing anything official – unless I'm in America? At a rodeo!

And what about Number 7?

NO GLITTER?

Seriously???

And Number 8?

Alice has to approve **ANY CUSTOMIZING** I do to my own clothes???

I sit silently, as I reread the guide, hoping I somehow missed the fun part.

But there is no fun part! It's only rules, rules, rules. Royal Rules and itchy fabrics.

MY LIFE IS SO OVER!!!

"But, Alice, this list is so…so…*unfair*! I mean, why can't I wear glitter? **I LOVE GLITTER!** And no jeans?"

"You'll have lots of lovely dresses and trouser suits, you'll see."

"But I don't want to wear lovely dresses and trouser

suits. I want to wear clothes I like and have chosen myself! Maybe even some I've made." I lean back and try to take some deep breaths. "How am I supposed to express who I am if I have to follow all of these rules?"

"But that is the point," Alice says. "You will be expressing exactly who you are: a princess and future queen of a country. And by following a predictable style—"

"It's *too* predictable! Zoë's wardrobe has more options and she's a guinea pig! I thought turning fourteen was going to be exciting but all it is is more **RULES**!" I jump up and start pacing the room.

"Calm down, Lily. These *guidelines* will keep you looking professional – and ensure that Waldenburgers can easily spot you in a crowd, something that is crucial when people have travelled long distances or stood outside for hours, waiting to see you."

"But surely if I'm wearing, say, my favourite customized denim jacket – one with sequins and embroidered patches all over it – they won't miss me? They might even notice me more!"

"Perhaps. But you need to draw attention to yourself in the right way, Lily – a way that shows dignity, both for what you represent and for the effort made by those who are hosting you. If people are distracted because of your dazzling clothes, they won't pay full attention to what you say and do. You need to keep everyone focused on the issues you will deal with as Crown Princess – nothing else matters. Certainly not making a fashion statement."

"But—"

"No buts, Lily – listen to Alice, she's correct." Grandmaman has swept into the room and is suddenly standing in front of the fireplace. She is wearing a purple dress with matching coat and hat. A large diamond brooch in the form of a flower is pinned to her coat; a small classic black handbag hangs on her wrist. I watch as she sets her handbag down, removes her gloves, coat and then her hat. She quickly runs her hands over her hair then turns to join us. I stand up to greet her while Alice pours her a drink.

"Now where were we?" she says as she sits down and motions for Alice and me to sit down, too. "Ah, yes, you were giving Alice a hard time about your new wardrobe guidelines. But I'm afraid there is nothing we can do about it, Lily. Dressing to fulfil the obligations of your role is very different from dressing to go out with your friends."

"But it's not fair! I should be able to decide what I'm going to wear!"

"You can decide everything – but it must follow the court guidelines. And there will be no more discussion about the matter. Now do you want to hear my surprise? I have an exciting idea I'm sure you will love…"

I'm sure it must be about me designing my ballgown – I could really use some good news…

I watch as Grandmaman takes a sip of her drink and looks at my sketches, which are still lying on the sofa.

"These are all lovely, Lily. And seeing them last week made me think about your talent and how much fashion means to you…which, in turn, made me think that perhaps I could find a fun fashion project for you, something that might help you develop your design skills. And I believe I have found just the project…"

Finally! I'm so excited!

"So your parents and I would be delighted if you would design…"

OMG!!! Ballgown designs are practically dancing in front of my eyes!

"…the new uniforms for the palace gardeners."

I'm about to yell, **"YAY!"** when I stop myself.

Did Grandmaman just say what I think she said? I must have heard wrongly… "Grandmaman, did you say *uniforms for the palace gardeners*?"

"I did!" she answers with a broad smile.

I'm in **TOTAL SHOCK**.

"But gardeners' uniforms **ARE NOT FASHION**!"

"There's no need to shout, Lily."

"But I thought you said a **FUN** project! A **FASHION** project."

"But this *is* a fun fashion project. And you'll develop your talent and create something practical at the same time. We haven't had new gardeners' uniforms designed since…well…since your mother became queen. I'm sure you'll come up with something splendid."

This is **THE WORST PRINCESS CLASS EVER**!

"But I don't want to design gardeners' uniforms! I don't want to wear itchy fabric or give up glitter. And I definitely don't want to follow a ton of rules! I want to—"

"Lily, please. I understand that uniforms and ballgowns are two very different things – but a good designer should be able to turn their hand to anything. I also understand that you are surprised to be starting your royal duties now, but you must start actively preparing for your role of Crown Princess – and *dressing appropriately is a part of that.*"

I'm angry and frustrated and I suddenly feel tears well up behind my eyes. Why can't I ever do anything I want to do? Why? Apart from riding Cupcake and vlogging? And my vlog is **SECRET** or I wouldn't even be allowed to do that! Being a princess is so **NOT** easy-peasy and I've had enough!

I scoop up my sketches and leave the room, Coco at my heels. I can hear Grandmaman calling after me but I don't care. I wouldn't even care if they threw me into the old dungeons!

Chapter THREE

7.08 p.m., in my bedroom

I run all the way back to my bedroom where I message Leonie and tell her the news.

> **Leonie:** What happened to designing your ballgown?

> **Me:** Wouldn't I like to know?!!
> Grandmaman didn't mention it at all!
> We only discussed the Royal Rules.
> How will I be able to get out of them?

> **Leonie:** It doesn't sound like there's much

you can do… Although I do agree with one of them: you do need a new Waldenburg national costume. The one you have now looked a bit small when you wore it at Easter. By next spring the skirt will be so short you'll be showing off your pants. Won't the palace love that!

Me: Ha ha. Very funny.

Leonie: Seriously, though, we have to come up with a plan… I mean, there has to be a way around all those Royal Rules…and we have to talk your mum and grandmother into letting you design at least one ballgown!

Me: I TOTALLY agree. Then I could make a second, secret ballgown in a different colour for Tiara Girl. Viewers would love it – especially if I can come up with something that is easy to make.

> Oops! I have to go – I can hear someone coming. I'll call you later.

The footsteps stop outside my room and I hear a gentle tapping on my door. I don't answer and after a moment my parents walk in.

I'm sitting on my beanbag, my eyes glued to my phone. Zoë is running around on the floor and Coco is lying on the beanbag with me.

"Lily," Mum starts, "I hear that your Princess Class didn't go so well tonight. Do you want to talk about it?"

I have to admit that when I finally put my phone down and glance up at Mum she looks beautiful, even in her palace-approved outfit. And although she isn't wearing a crown or tiara she still looks very regal. She is wearing a one-shouldered, long, red dress with delicate beads sewn all over it. Her shoes are strappy silver sandals with high heels. And her long reddish-blonde hair is pulled back in a low bun – all the better to show off her magnificent ruby and diamond necklace and matching chandelier earrings.

36

And Dad looks very handsome. His dark hair is slicked back and he is in black tie, which makes most men resemble penguins, but not my dad.

Okay, so maybe *they* can be glamorous when they follow the Royal Rules…but they're not thirteen!

"It is totally unfair!" I yell from my beanbag. "Like, I don't know **ANYONE** else who has to follow as many rules as I do – and Leonie totally agrees. Not only do I have to give speeches in front of a thousand people and say and do all the right things to all the right people, but I can't even wear glitter or customize my clothes. No this, no that! **NO FUN!!!** I already wear a uniform to school – and now I have to wear one to be a princess, too. And, then, just when I thought Grandmaman was going to ask me to design my birthday ballgown, instead she asks me to design **GARDENING UNIFORMS!!!** She knows I've never designed a uniform in my life! I've had enough: I don't want to be a princess and **I NEVER WANT TO BE A QUEEN!!!**"

Mum appears surprisingly calm and Dad seems concerned but I think he's also smiling just a little, which really annoys me. It's like they aren't taking me seriously!

I pretend to pick a thread off my furry beanbag as I fight against the tear pushing its way to the corner of my eye. It's embarrassing when you're trying to make a point to your parents and you have to stop yourself from crying like a baby.

Mum leans down towards me. "Lily, I know exactly how you feel."

"NO, YOU DON'T!"

"Please don't shout – and yes, I do. Believe me. I went through exactly what you are going through now. Do you think it was any different for me? I, too, was the heir to the throne, and my life, too, was dictated by the court and the palace and Grandmaman. The 'Royal Rules' I used to call them."

I stare up at Mum in surprise. "That's what I call them."

Mum laughs. "I'm not surprised. Goodness, they infuriated me. When I was your age the only time I ever felt free was when I was riding my pony, Firefly."

That's funny because that's exactly how I feel, too,

when I ride Cupcake. The only other thing that makes me feel free is secretly vlogging. But I can't tell Mum about Tiara Girl because the last thing I want is to risk being labelled a Royal Rebel and having it shut down. Instead I say, "Really? You never told me that."

"Well, it's the truth."

"But I bet you didn't have Princess Class!"

Mum smiles and nods. "I did. With Baroness Marie-Julie de Saint-Saverne. She was one of Grandmaman's ladies-in-waiting – and she was much stricter than Alice."

"I don't believe it!"

Mum laughs. "You have it easy with Alice. Marie-Julie was a nightmare."

"It doesn't feel like I have it easy."

"I know, Lily, but it is important that you understand your destiny—"

"But there are so many rules! I'm going to change all of them when I'm queen!"

Dad is nodding his head gently, but Mum is suddenly very serious. "If only it was that easy! Lily, being a queen and running a country is a lot of work.

Everything you do or say is scrutinized by the press and the public. You must consider the needs of your queendom at all times, make some very big decisions, and lead by example... I very rarely get to do what I want."

"So why do it?"

"Because we love our country." Mum pauses for a moment. "And because Waldenburg is a very special place. As you know, it is the only queendom in the world... There is no other country where girls and women have as much choice and power over their own lives. So I believe we have an obligation to show the world that girls and women are strong and capable, both as leaders and citizens – *and*, believe it or not, dressing in a professional manner helps us get our message across."

"But what does it matter whether I wear a perfect princess dress or something fun that I've customized or designed? I'm still Lily Waldenburg!"

"Of course, Lily, you *can* always wear what you want...but the question is: will it serve your purpose? As I'm sure Alice explained, if your outfit is super fashionable and attention-grabbing it can, unfortunately, draw focus away from your good work. People will end up taking more notice of your clothes than hearing what you say... You need to be remembered for your words and actions – not your fashion choices. Does that make sense?"

I think hard about what Mum has just said and I do understand. Sort of...

Dad suddenly chimes in. "You know, I had to learn all this, too. I went to Prince Class before I married your mother..."

Holy royal macaroni! This day is full of more surprises than there are turrets on the castle. Dad laughs when he sees my expression.

"As you know I was an athlete when I met your mum" – **FYI**: Dad was on the Mexican ski team and met Mum when he came to Waldenburg to compete in the Winter Olympics – "and I come from a 'normal' background. I had no idea which fork to use at six-course dinners, or what to wear to open a new hospital, or how I should address heads of state and other royalty."

"So who taught you Prince Class?"

Mum and Dad shout, "Alice!" at the same time.

Wow. Poor Dad!

"And keep in mind," Dad continues, "that when I moved here I had to learn Waldenburgerish, so to 'help' me Alice only spoke to me in Waldenburgerish during my Prince Class. It was a nightmare!"

While I digest all of this information Mum is quiet. But then Dad glances at his watch and says, "We have to go, the guests are arriving. The French and German Ministers of Economy are having dinner with us tonight. Well, them and about forty other European ministers." Dad smiles. "Good thing I had all those Prince Classes, so I'll know how to behave myself." Then he winks at me.

As Mum heads to the door she stops and turns. "Lily, I came to tell you that I really would appreciate it if you would design new uniforms for the palace gardeners." Mum raises her hand when she sees me start to say something. "I know you may not believe me now, but I'm sure that designing the uniforms will be a *fun* project that you will enjoy once you start.

And if we end up using your design we can post a picture of it on the Royal Court's official social media accounts, and draw some attention to your talent – you've always wanted to be on Instagram."

"Mum, I know you're trying to help me but there is **NOTHING FUN** about designing gardening uniforms."

"Well then, maybe you'll like this idea: if you can come up with a really practical and chic design for the palace gardeners then we – your father, Grandmaman and I – agree that you can design the ballgown for your birthday ball."

Mum is not joking – I can tell because she is not smiling and she is observing me with an arched eyebrow – a sign that she is serious.

But still I have to ask: "Really and truly, cross your heart?"

Mum nods. "But I will have to approve your design."

I think about this for a moment but quickly decide that I can totally live with it.

"YAYAYAYAYAYYAYAY!!!"

I jump up and hug Mum and Dad, and Coco is barking, and I'm so excited I can't stop jumping. Until I remember something important. I turn to Mum and lightly blow into my right palm, then I hold out my hand. "If you really promise then we have to do a special handshake."

Mum looks down at her right hand, which is perfectly manicured with dark red nail varnish and has two enormous diamond rings on it. Then she also blows into her palm and shakes my hand.

We have a royal deal.

I would have loved for Leonie to come over to the palace tonight for dinner so that we could discuss all of this, but when you live in a palace, your friends can't just hop on their bicycles and drop by – especially not when your mum has forty or so European ministers downstairs for dinner. Even when there isn't something special going on, security are always on the alert. The palace has to know who's coming over, their name must be on the visitor list and they must bring proper identification. If they get past all of that, then they will be escorted in. It's different when Leonie walks back to the palace with me after school because then she's *with me*. Otherwise, even she can't just walk up to the gates and knock.

See what I mean?

Not so easy-peasy.

So on my way down to dinner (just me and Coco – in the small dining room) I message Leonie instead.

Me: I get to design my birthday ballgown!!! I talked to my mum and it's all sorted! Well, sort of... I have to design the gardeners' uniforms first, then I can design my ballgown...

Leonie: Yay! That's fab news! Do you have any ideas for the uniforms yet?

An image of the current outfit springs to mind: polo shirt and trousers in olive green with brown trim; a crown with my mum's monogram underneath it, embroidered in red thread, decorates the shirt pockets. It's safe, boring and palace-approved – and gives me the design zzzzs.

> Me: No… All I know is that they have to be practical. They need pockets large enough for small gardening tools and they have to be comfortable enough to work in all day. Oh, plus, the fabric has to be thick enough to handle rose thorns.

> Leonie: That doesn't sound that simple…

> Me: Tell me about it! But Mum and Grandmaman say that a designer should be able to design anything…and I guess they have a point. Anyway, I have to come up with a good concept…or no ballgown.

> Leonie: Don't worry – I'm sure you'll have a brilliant idea soon.

Me: I royally hope so!

We agree to meet first thing in the morning at the school gates to chat more. We also decide to come back to the palace together after school so that we can film my next Tiara Girl video. I have some super-exciting ideas and I know Leonie – and my viewers – will love them.

YAY!

I eat dinner alone (peanut-butter cheesecake for dessert – **LOVE!**) because my parents and Grandmaman are at the dinner downstairs. So on the way back to my bedroom, I make a detour through a service door halfway down a long passageway. It leads to a wooden staircase, at the top of which is a small door. As I gently turn the handle, I put my finger to my lips and tell Coco to keep quiet.

We very quietly slide through the door and step onto a narrow balcony that runs just below the large domed ceiling of the Tapestry Hall. I lean over the railing and peer down. The huge hall is buzzing with the sounds of conversation and laughter. My mother

47

and father sit opposite each other in the middle of a very long table decorated with massive flower arrangements from the palace greenhouses. The polished silver and crystal glitter in the candlelight – but even from this distance Mum's jewels sparkle the most. I can spot Alice, dressed in a powder-blue gown, and Grandmaman in pink.

I look left and right, and nod to the soldiers lined up along the balcony on either side of me. They are from the Queen's Royal Rosenheim Regiment Band, here to provide music throughout the dinner.

The soldiers aren't surprised to see me because I've been sneaking onto this balcony since I was a little girl when my nanny, Sandra, would bring me here.

Tonight, for the first time, though, as I look at the scene below, I can't help thinking that some day I will have to sit at the table as hostess – and queen.

Clearly my Princess Classes are having some effect!

I just hope that when the day comes I'll be able to do the job as well as Mum... I mean, Mum makes it looks so easy as she glides around the palace and in and out of Parliament. And while I want to be able to do the job and make Waldenburgers proud, I also don't want to stop doing everything I love, like vlogging and making my **DIY** fashion. Surely I can find a way to be both myself *and* a queen, too?

I royally hope so...

Chapter FOUR

11.27 a.m., Tuesday, at school

Leonie and I are walking down the main corridor of our school when she nudges me. "Don't look now but Max is heading towards us – and it looks like he wants to talk to you."

As if I don't have enough on my mind. The last person I need to meet right now is Max, leader of our school's Boys' Movement and the person I gave a royal lecture to on the school steps last week, after he nearly caused another student to be run over.

"Umm…Lilian." He looks nervous and I keep expecting him to whip out a sign about gender equality and start yelling my name, because until this moment that is all he's ever done when he sees me. "Or do you prefer to be called Lily?"

"It's Your Royal Highness, actually, Max."

"Umm…okay. Your—"

"I'm kidding. Lily is fine. I'm just happy that you seem to have left the signs at home. I'm assuming you haven't scared any more students into the path of a moving vehicle."

Max turns bright red.

"Actually that's why I'm stopping you. I didn't get a chance to say thank you properly last week after, after…well, you know. I also wanted to say I'm sorry. I didn't mean to harass you with my chanting and following you around and stuff…" Max turns even redder. "Umm…maybe from now on we can discuss things properly – like, without the sign-waving and flyers?" Max holds out his hand.

"Sure." We shake hands.

"Good. Because there is a lot that needs to be changed in this country." Max is walking beside me now. I'd prefer it if he didn't – Leonie and I still haven't had the chance to talk about my uniform ideas yet –

but it wouldn't be polite to brush him off after he just apologized.

"Waldenburg is way behind the times when it comes to gender equality."

"Hmm...that may be, Max. But then again, it depends on how you look at it. In most of the rest of the world, the balance of power is heavily tipped in favour of boys." I can't believe this answer just flows out of me; if only Alice could hear me now!

"Yeah, well...I can only say that as a boy living here, it's not always easy. I mean, take our school plays, for example." He looks pointedly at Leonie as he makes this comment, all sign of his earlier embarrassment gone. (**FYI**: Max is in the school Drama Club and Leonie always gets the leads.)

I feel Leonie tense beside me, but before she can answer him we reach the classroom and Max has to go – which is a relief, because Leonie and I have a **MAJOR FASHION DESIGN ISSUE** to discuss.

Okay, so maybe it's more of a *uniform* design issue...but if I think of it as a *fashion* design issue I'm sure I'll feel more inspired.

At least I hope so...

Later, in Art class, we are supposed to be doing black and white drawings using a technique called "pointillism". Monsieur Falck, our teacher, is busy with a group of students at the opposite side of the classroom, so I pick up a pencil and try to sketch a gardener's uniform, but not one single idea flows from my pencil.

"I'm having trouble," I whisper to Leonie. "At this rate I'll never get to design my own ballgown!"

"Maybe your brain needs some fertilizer in order to be productive. Get it? It's a gardening joke! Ha ha!"

"Very funny."

"Seriously, though, maybe you should do some research..."

"Research into gardening uniforms?"

Leonie nods as she adds some dots to her mother's nose – not that Leonie's portrait looks *anything* like Mrs Leonberger. I don't say this to Leonie, though. Instead I take out my phone and search. But all that comes up are pictures of gardeners dressed in polo shirts and loose work trousers in green, or brown, or both – just like the uniforms the palace gardeners already have.

Regardless, I lift my pencil and try a few sketches. I start by drawing the existing uniforms from memory. Then I redo the outlines, making the legs of the trousers more fitted, then the polo shirts. But no matter what I do my efforts leave me feeling uninspired. I try a few different trouser shapes and get nowhere. I'm stuck. I quickly draw a ballgown, just to make myself feel better.

"Any luck?" Leonie whispers.

I shake my head. "Any time I start to get excited about an idea, I suddenly remember that the uniforms have to be used by women *and* men – plus, they have to be comfortable, have large pockets for walkie-talkies and other tools, and made of strong, thick fabric. There are so many rules that it's kind of squashing my creativity…"

The only good thought I have is that the uniform should be the exact same colour green as the green on the Waldenburg flag. (Our national flag is green and white with my family's coat of arms – a white unicorn rearing against a red shield – smack in the middle of it. It's super cool!)

But other than this, I don't have **ONE SINGLE IDEA**.

Which means I'm no closer to designing my ballgown than I was this morning. I sigh and concentrate on finishing my pointillism portrait of Cupcake.

Usually I ride Cupcake when I get home from school but this afternoon she is having new shoes put on, so I can't. This actually works out well, though, because Leonie and I have to do our homework and then Leonie is going to help me film my next Tiara Girl video.

Coco comes rushing out to greet us as we enter the palace grounds. Sandra (who used to be my nanny but nowadays looks after my clothes and helps me pack my bags when I travel and basically checks on everything I do) always lets Coco out at this time of day because otherwise she sits and whines in the main hall. She can make a lot of noise.

Together the three of us (plus my palace security, so make that six) walk across the gardens to the palace. I smile and wave at every gardener we pass, carefully examining their uniforms as I do.

"Why don't you forget about the gardeners' uniforms for the rest of the day?" Leonie suggests, opening the side door. "I've read that if you try too hard to be creative you can sometimes make your brain tired – like writer's block. But if you give your brain a break and focus on a totally different and random task, then – abracadabra! – it will suddenly come up with the perfect idea by itself. It's all part of the creative process. Trust me, I know – I'm an actor."

Sometimes Leonie's ideas can sound far-fetched, but they often work. I decide to follow her advice. After all, it's not as if thinking about it has worked so far.

So, instead, we race to my bedroom to discuss the outfit I'm going to film for my next Tiara Girl video.

And I can't help but notice how easily the ideas flow when it's something I've made and designed for *myself*.

Our homework finished, Leonie and I are free to go up to my turret and film. But first, I have to get my outfit and props together. So I head to my walk-in wardrobe and find a pair of dungarees that I designed and sewed this summer – although, as soon as I realized I wanted to film them, I added some gorgeous new glittery patches and embroidery to them just last weekend.

Royal Confession: I can't sew *that* well – I'm much better at customizing – as I only started learning in the spring, after Grandmaman gave me a sewing machine for Christmas last year. But I have taught myself how to make dungarees (they're easy) and I'm really good at creating dresses using tulle (that's the fabric used on ballet tutus) because it's so fluffy that I can hide any mistakes just by stitching another layer on. Speaking of which, I'm super lucky that

Mum and Grandmaman's dressmakers give me their fabric offcuts.

I've decided to make this video about dungarees because I wore them in one of my videos (Vlog #2: Get Your Pony Glitzed Out – Tiara Girl Style!) and got a massive response from viewers asking questions about where I bought them or how I customized them. And I even have the perfect title for this video: **Tiara Girl's Top Tips for Designing Dreamy Dungarees.**

Along with my dungarees, I make sure to gather up a few props to include in the video, like my paper patterns and design sketches. Once I have everything I'll need, I open my bedroom door and peer left and right down the corridor. I wait a moment, but I don't hear any footsteps and I don't see any approaching shadows. The coast is clear! With Coco beside me and Zoë in my rucksack, I signal to Leonie to follow me. I leave the music playing and the lights on in my bedroom, so that it seems like we're still inside… You see, my turret room is a **SECRET** – *and it needs to stay a secret…*

I bet you're wondering why I need a secret room?

Especially when I live in a palace and already have a bedroom – plus hundreds of other rooms (about eight hundred according to Grandmaman) that I can use at any time.

ANSWER: Because it is the only room where I can be **TOTALLY ALONE!**

Okay, so I understand that security's role is to protect me – so I'm not kidnapped or whatever – but sometimes I just want to escape the eyes that follow my every move. Outside the palace, it's specially trained police protection. But even inside the palace, there are a **TON** of people always looking out for me: Alice, my parents and Grandmaman, of course, but also butlers, footmen, cleaners, lady's maids, florists, chefs – even the clock-winder.

Basically I'm always being watched.

When I mentioned this to Alice she said, "It will be worse the day you become queen."

Alice is so **NOT** understanding!

With so many people around me all the time, filming videos for a secret vlog is very challenging. Which is why I was thrilled when I discovered my

59

secret turret room totally by accident. I can leave all of my Tiara Girl stuff there, without worrying that Sandra or Alice or Mum will find it or walk in on me while I'm filming and ask what is going on.

I quietly shut the door of my bedroom then head down the corridor. I stop when we reach an old Flemish tapestry hanging on the wall. It is large and heavy so I carefully lift the edge of the side nearest me then slip behind it. Once we're all underneath we shuffle along, until we reach a secret door that has been painted to match the stone wall; at waist level a tiny golden knob juts out from it. I turn it and push and we walk through.

I flip the switch on the wall to my left and some of the old light bulbs in the golden torches lining the stairwell flicker to life. I sweep my eyes upwards: the spiral staircase winds on and on, all the way to my turret at the top.

When I first found my secret turret it looked like it hadn't been dusted in about a hundred years – there were cobwebs everywhere! The only things inside it were a large armchair, a gold mirror and a desk (all of

which I use). The heavy gold key, which I now keep in a special box under my bed, was still in the lock. I've never heard Grandmaman or Mum or Dad or even Alice mention this tower, so it must have been forgotten about long ago.

About a week ago I filmed a special **DIY** decorating video in my turret: Tiara Girl's Tips for Your Own DIY Room. It was the best video! I had so much fun making it because Leonie and I came up with every single idea in it ourselves *and* we even made the whole video together. Leonie filmed me while I jazzed the room up with pink paint, fairy lights, a mood board and lots of really **CUTE** pictures that I hung up to form the shape of a big heart.

As soon as Leonie and I reach my turret I change into my dungarees and Leonie starts setting up the lighting.

"Ta-dah!" I say after I change and spin round in front of her. They are dark blue and embellished with loads of sparkly patchwork butterflies and hearts. They look royally awesome!

"**OMG!!!** They look even better on. I love the

butterflies!" Leonie puts some music on and we start to dance. After a few minutes of spinning and twirling, I put my pink wig and heart-shaped sunglasses on and, hey presto – I'm Tiara Girl!

I have to wear a disguise when I film my Tiara Girl videos – after all, it's the best way to keep viewers from guessing that I'm actually the **CROWN PRINCESS OF WALDENBURG**!

While Leonie sets up the lights and camera, I take my sketches and the patterns I made for the dungarees out of my rucksack. Zoë has already climbed out and is squealing contentedly as she runs back and forth across the floor of the round room. I lift her up and take her to the window so she can admire the view – having short legs shouldn't mean she can't enjoy it.

My turret is the highest one on the castle. The palace and the craggy mountaintop it sits on fall away steeply on this side, down to the beautiful green valley far below – the Valley of the Queens. Seen from here the town looks like a tiny fairy-tale model and it's almost hard to believe it's real.

"You can't let Zoë admire the view for ever, you

know, or someone might start wondering where we are," Leonie suddenly says. "We don't have a second to waste."

She has a point. I set Zoë down and get ready to start filming.

There are three main points that I want to cover in **Tiara Girl's Top Tips for Designing Dreamy Dungarees:**

1. Dungarees are really cool and super versatile and can be worn almost anywhere, from music festivals to mucking out your pony's stall, and from fun parties to lounging around the house.
2. They are quite simple to make. To prove this, I'll show the paper patterns I used.
3. They are easy-peasy to customize with patches and embroidery because they have so many flat areas of fabric. On dungarees you can really go crazy with the **DIY** decoration!

I lay out my patterns and sketches on the large desk then quickly brush my pink wig. Now for the tiara…

I always wear some kind of tiara in my videos – after all, I call my vlog *Tiara* Girl. Mostly, they have been **DIY** ones – with the super-shiny exception of my last video, when I wore a **REAL** one! For this video I'd like to use something different from my usual DIY crystal ones, so instead I'm using something that I made a couple of weeks ago. It's not a tiara in the usual sparkly sense – it's actually a flower crown. It's made of colourful silk flowers and it looks **AMAZING!!!** There are small daisies, pink roses, blue cornflowers, violets, white peonies and yellow buttercups – it's a floral explosion!

I bought the bag of mixed flowers at the craft shop in town and then glued them onto a plastic headband. A cute flower crown like this is a quick way to add some fun to almost any outfit.

Leonie stops fiddling with the lights and inspects my look. "I love your flower crown. But…hmm…" She peers at me through half-closed eyes, her arms crossed in front of her. "You need a touch more blusher. The

lighting is stronger than usual today, in order to pick up the colourful butterfly patches against the dark blue of your dungarees. So you'd better put a bit more colour on your cheeks or you'll look like Count Eberhart's ghost in your video."

FYI: Count Eberhart is the palace ghost! He runs along the castle ramparts seeking revenge (he was killed when his plot to take the queendom from one of my ancestors was discovered) and legend says he will one day strike down a Waldenburg queen. I royally hope it won't be me.

Another **FYI**: Leonie is a genius with these details. It's really practical having a **BFF** who is on her way to becoming a major movie star, because she knows all about lighting and camera angles.

"As an actor I have to be aware of what happens behind the camera, too, you know," she points out.

I can't argue with that.

Finally we start filming and I have a feeling this video is going to look **SO** cool! We get close-ups of all the embroidery work I've done – plus some of my butterfly and heart patches. We also get close-ups of

Zoë, who is wearing a tiny collar that matches my flower tiara. I made hers with the tiniest flowers from the bagful I bought.

In the video I talk about the paper patterns I made and then show viewers how they can measure how much fabric they'll need to make their own dungarees.

I sign off with a close-up of me saying, "Dungarees are super fun and super practical and I think every Tiara Girl needs a pair in their wardrobe. Wishing you a glitter-filled week of happiness and amazing **DIY**!!! Until next time…"

Leonie yells, "Cut!" (She likes to use professional film terms to prepare for her career as a movie star.) I quickly change and gather up my stuff while Leonie turns off the lights, then we rush back down to my bedroom unnoticed.

Two minutes later there's a knock at my door. I quickly push my pink Tiara Girl wig and my heart-shaped sunglasses under my bed, then Leonie hands me a face wipe and I remove as much of my camera-ready make-up as I can before the door opens.

Leonie and I stand and smile and try to look as if we have **NOTHING** to hide.

It's Sandra. For what seems like an age Sandra carefully looks us over and I cross my fingers behind my back, hoping that she doesn't notice anything odd.

She doesn't.

PHEW!

Instead she says, "Princess Lily, Countess Vendelstein has asked me to tell you that Professor Waltraud Hustemeier is still feeling unwell. Furthermore, because the Countess is with your parents at an important event this evening she will be unable to step in for Professor Hustemeier and, therefore, she must cancel this evening's Princess Class."

I want to yell, **"YAY!"** – but I stop myself in time because it wouldn't be very nice of me, considering that Professor Hustemeier is feeling unwell, so instead I calmly say, "Okay. Thank you."

Sandra continues, "However, the Queen Mother has asked that you join her for dinner at 7 p.m. And" – Sandra turns towards Leonie – "she has asked whether Miss Leonberger would like to come too? You will, of course, be driven back home afterwards."

Leonie says she'd love to have dinner with Grandmaman and me, and Sandra says she will call Leonie's parents to let them know.

Before she leaves, Sandra suggests that I put a nice dress on – as if I'm ten years old! She even pulls one out of my wardrobe that she deems suitable, then suggests I wear a pair of shoes I don't like – they are dull green and have a buckle. A buckle! Sandra thinks they're beautiful. That's what happens when you live in Fashion Siberia (aka Waldenburg).

I nod yes but ignore her advice and wear a cute customized dress, plus a pair of my customized trainers. Grandmaman won't mind – as long as my hair is brushed. Grandmaman's pet peeve is unbrushed hair – she says it's not "neat" and that, "a princess must always look neat, if nothing else".

That must be Royal Rule Number 2,009, I think to myself.

Ha ha ha ha ha!

I'd laugh more except it's probably true.

Chapter FIVE

6.55 p.m., in the small dining room

Royal **FYI**: if you have a meeting with a queen – even if she is a "retired" queen and, by the way, also your grandmother – you must always arrive before she does. According to palace rules, it is super impolite to make a queen (or king or president or any head of state) wait. Alice is very strict about this.

By running the length of the ballroom at top speed, Leonie and I arrive well before Grandmaman and even have time to smooth our hair with our hands.

Grandmaman walks in and I'm about to greet her and Leonie is about to curtsy, when we both freeze and our mouths drop open: Grandmaman is covered, head to toe, in pearls.

I am not kidding.

There are three diamond and pearl bracelets on each wrist, pearl rings on her fingers, a five-strand pearl choker with a huge sapphire clasp around her neck, plus a long chain of pearls that reaches her hips, a pair of enormous pearl drop earrings and, last, but not least, a very grand pearl-and-diamond tiara on her head that's nearly the size of a crown!

"It's okay, Lily, you can close your mouth now." Grandmaman greets us and continues, "I had a meeting today with Baron de Reedtz" – he's the Master of the Crown Jewels – "and he is worried that the pearls in the Royal Collection are not getting worn enough."

She notices my confusion.

"Pearls, Lily, are the product of living things; unlike stones, they require regular contact with human skin to keep their lustre. Apparently ours are looking a bit dull – they need to be worn more often. So I said I'd help."

"Do you have to wear them for ever?"

"No, just this week. I'll wear different pieces whenever I'm home for the evening. That should be enough to help with their lustre. And then we'll have to be sure to wear them more often, in general."

"Will you sleep with all of that on?"

"Yes. Well, not the tiara, obviously, or the earrings. I will remove them after dinner. But as for the rest," – Grandmaman holds her arms out and looks down the front of her dress – "I doubt the necklaces and bracelets will bother me very much, so, yes, I will try to sleep with them on. Take note, Lily, because one day you'll have to do the same... They're lovely, aren't they?" she suddenly says to Leonie, who is staring at her earrings. "They were a gift from the Russian ambassador of Catherine the Great's court."

"Maybe I can help give them back their lustre, too," Leonie suggests. "I could take one of the tiaras home tonight in my rucksack, wear it around the house and then take it to school tomorrow. We could put it in your locker while we're in class," Leonie says as she turns to me.

"Thank you, Leonie." Grandmaman smiles. "I'd love to accept your help but I'm not sure the palace security would agree. However" – Grandmaman has a twinkle in her eye now – "I'm sure they won't mind if I do this..." We watch as she slips one diamond-and-pearl bracelet off each of her wrists and hands them to Leonie and me to wear for dinner. Leonie and I can hardly take our eyes off them and I keep raising my glass very high just so I can see my bracelet catch the soft candlelight of the dinner table.

"That's enough, Lily," Grandmaman finally says. "A princess does not keep her arm raised throughout the whole of dinner."

"Is that another Royal Rule? Ha ha!" But Grandmaman just frowns, and my joke falls as flat as the crêpes Suzette being served for dessert.

As I'm finishing off the orange sauce with my dessert spoon, Grandmaman says, "Ah! Before I forget, there was one thing I promised Alice I'd tell you tonight, Lily, and that is that, as preparation for your birthday ball, you will start waltz lessons tomorrow."

WHAT!?!? WALTZ LESSONS?

"But why?"

"Because, Lily, as you know, *you* must be the one to dance the first dance of your birthday ball. Royal tradition dictates it. Plus, your ball will be televised and Waldenburgers will expect you to make a graceful and confident impression as you come of age. All eyes will be on you."

Grandmaman looks totally calm as she drops this

ENORMOUS BOMBSHELL!!!

"But I thought I'd dance with Dad! And just follow his lead!" A piece of crêpe Suzette comes flying out of my mouth and shoots across the table.

"Lily, please calm down and remember not to speak if you have food in your mouth. And, yes, your *first* dance will be with your father and he is an excellent dancer—"

"Perfect – I don't need classes then."

"That might work...except that after your first dance you will have to dance with the Crown Prince of Denmark, the King of Spain, the President of the United States, the King of Jordan—"

"Are you serious?" Leonie and I both ask at the same time.

"Absolutely. So please be in the ballroom at 6 p.m. tomorrow."

Out of the corner of my eye I see Leonie stifle a giggle. I'd probably be giggling, too, **IF IT WASN'T MY LIFE!!!**

"The ballroom? But it's huge and it'll be empty."

Grandmaman nods. "It will be full on your birthday – and practising in the same room will give you confidence on the day of the ball."

"And who am I supposed to dance with tomorrow? My shadow?"

"Don't be flippant, Lily." Grandmaman is not amused. "Your coming-of-age ball – the first since your mother's, thirty-one years ago – is a royal tradition that Waldenburgers are very proud of. Many people will be looking forward to helping us celebrate your special day. As for your partner, I believe a charming young man has been found."

A charming young man?!?!?

Honestly, I could cry. "Who?"

"I have no idea – but he's been chosen by Alice. She interviewed him yesterday."

Leonie can't stop giggling.

"If I can, I'll stop by and watch," Grandmaman says. "You'll love waltzing."

Why doesn't Grandmaman just throw me into the dungeons this very minute?

As we get up to leave, Grandmaman asks how my design for the gardeners' uniforms is coming along. "You only have two days, I'm afraid, Lily, or else we'll really have to pass the project on to a professional designer."

News of my waltz class and mystery dance partner has been such a shock to my system that it takes me a moment to calm down and clear my head... I don't want her to think that I have **ABSOLUTELY NO IDEA** what I'm going to design and haven't even come up with one good sketch, because I really, really want to design my birthday ballgown. Finally I say, "I'll have something to show you tomorrow at breakfast."

Leonie's eyebrows rise high in alarm but I ignore her.

"That's wonderful, Lily. I look forward to seeing it. If Valentino and Armani could design airline uniforms then I'm sure you will do a wonderful job for our gardeners."

I wish I felt as confident as she clearly does.

Grandmaman says goodnight to us and I take Leonie downstairs to the inner courtyard of the palace, where the chauffeur is waiting.

"I wonder who your dance partner is," Leonie says on our way down.

"Who knows? But I'll bet the Crown Jewels it's not someone I'd choose."

Leonie nods. "I know you get to wear a tiara and live in a palace and stuff…but, seriously, Lily, when I think of all the things you have to learn and how many rules you have to follow, I'm happy I'm *not* a princess."

"Ha ha. Thanks…" I kick a pebble across the courtyard as Coco looks up at me and wags her tail.

"Well, at least we filmed a really cute video tonight!"

"We did!"

"Listen…" Leonie is suddenly serious. "If I think

of any good ideas for a uniform I'll call you, okay?"

I nod and take a deep breath. "Why did I ever say I'd have one ready by tomorrow morning?"

"Don't worry, you will," Leonie reassures me. "I have a hunch you're about to get a really good idea."

"I hope so...I need one. The only thing that can make waltzing bearable is doing it in a gown I've designed myself!"

Leonie and I hug then quickly make up a new special handshake: I hold my hand out as if to shake hands normally except I'm actually holding my hand with my thumb pointing to the floor. Then we repeat the handshake but this time it's Leonie's thumb that's pointing down. We decide it means good luck. I watch as she gets in the waiting car and wave until it drives out of the courtyard. Then Coco and I race back to my bedroom.

It's time to design a uniform – and edit my next video!

Chapter SIX

9.08 p.m., in my bedroom

Tiara Girl's Top Tips for Designing Dreamy Dungarees looks amazing!!! I've edited the footage and added some cool graphics – fun words, flying butterflies, stars and flowers – as well as some music. I click to upload it to my channel then spring onto my bed and start jumping up and down on my mattress with Coco. **WEEHEEEE!!!** I'm so excited! The video is super fun and I hope viewers will feel inspired to make their own dungarees – they're just so stylish yet practical—

Practical…

As the word runs through my mind I stop jumping. Then I leap off my bed and grab my laptop. Quickly,

I rewind the video to the bit where I talk about how practical dungarees are and I feel I'm looking at them with new eyes, because suddenly I notice how perfect they could be for things like *raking* and *digging*. Plus, they have large pockets – which I use for sweets and Coco's tennis balls – but I bet they could just as easily hold a pair of secateurs…

I peer closer at my laptop screen.

How about if, instead of trying to create something similar to the existing uniforms, I design something that *I actually like*?

Something *I'd* want to wear?

Something like *dungarees*?

I'm so excited that I call Leonie to tell her my new idea.

"**OMG!** That is *the* best! And I bet your parents and grandmother will love it!"

I tell Leonie I'll see her at school and hang up. I don't have a minute to lose. I told Grandmaman I'd have a design to show her tomorrow morning – but what if instead of just a drawing, I show her a finished pair of dungarees?

I know I have an old pair, the first dungarees I ever made. If I can find them, I can customize them right now...

I rush to my wardrobe but Coco is quicker than me. Her tail is wagging so fast it's a blur; her nose is pressed against the cupboard door. "You're so clever, Coco! You always read my mind!" I tell her. I find the dungarees and lay them on my bed.

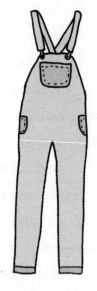

It seems like this idea is just meant to be, because the dungarees are green – maybe not the exact same green as on the Waldenburg flag, but they'll do for my morning presentation. After studying them for a few minutes I start having ideas about how I want to customize them...

First I go to my desk and find a permanent green marker. With this I cover all the golden brass bits on the dungarees so that they are tone-on-tone with the fabric. I think this makes the dungarees look less flashy, which I like because it will help make the detail I'm about to add pop even more...

I reach for the box under my bed, the one where I keep all sorts of extra bits of fabric. I open it and take out some pieces of white, red and yellow material.

With the special pencil I have that draws on cloth, I mark out the outline of a rearing unicorn on the white fabric – it looks like the one on our family coat of arms and the Waldenburg flag. Then I draw a shield on the red fabric and a crown on the yellow fabric.

Next I very carefully cut the shapes from the different fabrics, before placing them on the top half of the dungarees. I lay the red shield down first, place the unicorn on top of it and top it off with the crown. **IT LOOKS AMAZING!!!** I'm so excited I can hardly hold the needle and thread as I sew the fabric in place but I manage. Then I safety-pin the wide trouser legs back to give the dungarees a straight-legged silhouette – that will make it easier for the gardeners when they have to tuck them into their wellington boots.

As a last, useful touch – one that I'm sure Mum and Grandmaman will like – I decide to add some larger pockets to the dungarees. After I find some suitable green fabric in my box, I make a quick paper pattern of the size and shape I need the pockets to be. Using the pattern, I cut the material and quickly sew the new pockets onto the dungarees.

Unfortunately I don't have any zips in my supplies or I'd add them to the pockets, as a way of closing them, so the gardeners can, for instance, carry their walkie-talkies in them. But I figure I can explain this detail to Mum and Grandmaman during my presentation.

Finally, when I've done all I can for tonight, I put the dungarees on and stand in front of my full-length mirror.

Holy royal macaroni!!! They look **AWESOME!!!**

And practical.

And stylish! I mean, how many gardeners' uniforms have white unicorns on them?

None – **EXCEPT MINE!!!**

LOVE!!!

I notice a few last tiny details that need attention, though, so after I change out of the dungarees, I take a fine, black permanent marker and draw an eye on the unicorn's profile. I also add a few lines to its body, mane, tail and horn, along with a touch of shading. That looks much better so I add a bit of detail to the crown, too… It ends up looking amazing. I can't wait to show the dungarees to Grandmaman and my parents. I really, really hope they'll love my idea!

I go back to my wardrobe and look through my riding clothes. I think the dungarees would look best with a matching green polo shirt, so I find one and pull it out. I'll wear it to breakfast, under my dungarees, so that Grandmaman and my parents can see the full effect of my design idea.

YAY!!!

Before I hang the dungarees in my wardrobe I use a lint roller to remove any of Coco's hairs from them. I want them to look perfect for tomorrow morning's breakfast presentation.

Then I go online to see how **Tiara Girl's Top Tips for Designing Dreamy Dungarees** is doing and I let out a whoop of excitement when I see that in the fifty-three minutes since I uploaded it, it has had 1,773 views!

And masses of kind and thoughtful comments…

"**OMG**, I never thought dungarees could look so cool!"

"Dear Tiara Girl, I love your vlog!!! It's the best!"

"Tiara Girl, can I buy your dungarees?"

"What kind of sewing machine do you use?"

"Please make a video on how to make a flower crown! Please, please, please!"

"When are you going to do a live event? I am such a fan and would love to meet you!"

I take several minutes to answer as many questions as I can. There are so many I just don't have the time to do them all right now because I have to get into bed before Mum and Dad come up to say goodnight. It's still such a big surprise to me to have so many people watching my videos – I never expected it. Leonie says I have real fans now – which I guess is true because I'm starting to recognize the names of some people who visit my channel again and again.

Also, so many of the questions I'm asked are ones I used to have, like: what kind of scissors do I prefer? Or how did I learn to sew? Or what kind of paper do I

84

use to make my patterns? When I started customizing my clothes I wish I had had someone share their **DIY** tips with me...

The only comment that makes my stomach twist a bit is the one from the fan asking me to hold a live event so she can meet me – especially when I see that there is a whole string of replies, with other viewers asking for the same thing!

I sit quietly for a moment thinking about this, because the truth is...I probably won't ever be able to hold a Tiara Girl live event for fear of being found out! Especially after I officially begin my royal duties – I mean, my face will be online and on television all the time, so it'll be even harder to keep my secret identity under wraps! And how could I ever explain to Alice and the palace that, oh, by the way, I'm just going into town for a few hours to meet fans of my vlog.

This makes me feel sad because I'd love to meet my viewers...but it's impossible. And if the Tiara Girl community keeps growing isn't there more chance someone will figure out who I *really* am??? And then what will I do?

I mean, just the other day at school I overheard a few girls (from a younger class) talking about Tiara Girl and how much they love it. My vlog! It was so weird – and yet I was secretly thrilled, too. I walked past them with my head bent down and crossed my fingers that they wouldn't say something like, "Hey, Lily, you look like Tiara Girl!" – luckily they didn't.

I didn't think about any of this when I started my vlog. For me Tiara Girl was just a fun way to secretly share my **DIY** fashion with others who had the same interest. I had **NO** idea my videos would start going viral...

I take a deep breath and answer the comment by saying that at the moment my schedule does not allow me the time to meet fans but that I hope that one day it will.

I keep reading more comments and notice that my flower crown is really popular, so maybe my next video should be about how to make one?

Being Tiara Girl is royally exciting!!!

I'm in bed when I hear a soft knock on my door and a moment later Mum and Dad walk in. Even in the dark I can tell how glamorous they look. Mum's dress is floor-length and dark in colour. The tiny cape she is wearing over her shoulders has a pretty satin ribbon that is tied at her neck – and her hair is in an updo and decorated with some seriously blingy diamond clips. Dad looks like a movie star in his white tie ensemble. They tell me about the dinner they attended at the French Embassy this evening, in aid of a joint humanitarian effort by both countries. Mum gave a brilliant speech, says Dad.

"How about your design for the gardeners' uniforms? Have you hit on the right idea yet?" Mum asks.

"I'll show you at breakfast tomorrow morning," I say mysteriously.

"Great. I'm very curious. You can't tell me more?" Mum raises her eyebrows.

I shake my head. "No, I want my presentation to be a surprise."

Mum says she can't wait and then asks me how

dinner with Grandmaman went. They laugh when I tell them about the pearls. Then I ask Mum if she ever had to take waltz lessons.

"Of course I did, Lily. Every Crown Princess of Waldenburg must learn to waltz."

"Plus a few men, too," Dad chimes in. "Like me."

"You, too, Dad? But why? You were living in Mexico when you turned fourteen!"

Dad smiles. "I was – but on the evening of our wedding your grandparents held a big ball for your mum and me here, in the palace. And, as tradition dictates, the bride and groom must dance the first dance – a waltz. So I had to learn."

"Who did you practise with?"

"We practised together," Mum says.

"Can't you practise with me, Dad? Please! I don't want to learn with some random guy Alice and the palace have found for me."

"Your father is busy," Mum says. "And I'm sure Alice has found you a nice partner. I think it's someone from your school."

"From my school? Are you serious?"

Mum nods.

CAN MY LIFE GET ANY MORE ROYALLY EMBARRASSING?!?!?

"But I'll never live it down if everyone at school finds out I'm taking waltzing lessons!"

"Relax, Lily. They won't. But even if they do, you just have to think of it as one more royal duty you must fulfil in order to prepare for your role as queen. As you know, I have to start the first dance every year at the ball I host after Parliament opens. It's something you'll have to do regularly, too."

I roll onto my back and pull the duvet over my head. "I don't want to be a queen! I want to be a fashion designer!"

"But you can," Mum says. "Tomorrow you're going to show me a design for a gardening uniform and, if that goes well, you'll get to design your own ballgown."

"It's not the same thing…"

"Maybe not – but it's pretty close," Dad says smoothly. "Anyway, I'm sure you'll waltz beautifully, Lily. And I look forward to twirling you across the ballroom for your first dance."

"I'll have died of embarrassment by then."

My parents pull the duvet back and kiss me on my forehead, pat Coco, then leave.

I shut my eyes and try to get some royal zzzzs, which is no easy task when your life is becoming more embarrassing by the **SECOND!!!**

Chapter SEVEN

7.48 a.m., Wednesday, in my bedroom

Hi Tiara Girl! And welcome to your channel!

Your most recent video:

Tiara Girl's Top Tips for Designing Dreamy

Dungarees has had:

15,289 views

YAY!!!

That's amazing – especially as I only posted it late last night. And I see loads more fun and friendly new comments, too.

I close my laptop and quickly change into the polo shirt and customized dungarees. I check that every little detail looks as good as possible, because I really need to dazzle Grandmaman and Mum.

Before leaving my bedroom I put some fresh straw and a couple of muesli treats in Zoë's cage. She squeals excitedly as she comes out of her nest to see me and I'm sure she's wishing me good luck. I give her a quick pet, then, with Coco by my side, I leave for breakfast.

I'm so excited that I burst into the small dining room and nearly crash into one of the footmen carrying a tray.

"Lily!" Mum says. "Please slow down."

"A princess never rushes into a room," Grandmaman adds with a quick glance at her delicate jewelled watch. "And you're not even late – in fact, you're early. Why the rush, Lily? And – oh!" Grandmaman puts her glasses on while Mum pushes her chair back to get a better look at my outfit.

"Is that what you have in mind for the gardeners' uniforms?" Mum asks.

I nod and twirl in front of them both, then strut like a catwalk model from one end of the dining room to the other. As I sashay past the table I explain that dungarees are practical for winter and summer – and I make sure to put my hands in the pockets and explain how I'd like them to have zips. I also point out the narrow trouser leg which can easily fit in the gardeners' boots.

"It's a completely different look from the one they have now..." Grandmaman says. "Not that that matters..."

I cross my fingers, hoping that Mum and Grandmaman like my idea... *Please...please... please...*

"I think they're brilliant," Mum finally says. "Although we'll have to see what the gardeners think – they're the ones who have to work in them, after all..."

"They remind me of the uniform we had in my mother's time..." Grandmaman says. I stop in front of them both so they can see my handiwork up close. Grandmaman reaches out to feel the fabric.

"I'd like them to be made of a stronger material," I say. "And I want the shade of green to be the same as on our flag."

"Great idea," Mum says. "I love the coat of arms – that's a very nice detail, Lily." Grandmaman is now standing and peering closely at my dungarees.

"And I can see they are comfortable – you can move easily in them," Mum adds.

"And they have those wonderful pockets in front for the gardeners' tools. They are *practical*," Grandmaman says as she steps back to look at me. "You're so talented, Lily. If you weren't going to be a queen, I'd suggest you become a fashion designer."

I don't tell Grandmaman that those are my plans anyway – even if I am going to be a queen one day. Instead, I say, "So do I get to design my own ballgown? Do I? Please say yes!!!"

Grandmaman and Mum both take a deep breath and look at each other.

I can hardly breathe.

"I'll have to run it past the gardeners," Mum says. "Frau Hauschka in particular is keen to see it…" **(FYI**:

Frau Hauschka is our Head Gardener.) "The Master of the Household, too… Bear in mind that even if they like your design, it might need to be tweaked…

"But I think your design is lovely, Lily – you have clearly worked hard to fulfil the brief. And…" Mum pauses to look at Grandmaman before she continues, "as long as the gardeners are happy I have no objection. I agree with your grandmother, Lily: you have made an admirable effort."

"**SO**…?" I say while Mum and Grandmaman exchange another glance.

"Well," Mum finally says, "I think we have ourselves a deal: you can start designing your birthday ballgown."

Mum and Grandmaman are beaming at me.

"**YAYAYAYAYAYAY!!!**" I jump up and down and Coco starts to bark. I give Mum and Grandmaman each a huge hug and then do a few twirls around the table.

"How did you get the idea for dungarees?" Grandmaman suddenly asks.

The question stops me in my tracks – the last thing I can tell them is the truth.

"Umm…well…it just kind of came to me last night while I was in my room…" Which is true, actually – just not the *whole* truth. Then I add, "I decided to think about what *I* would like to wear – and not necessarily about all of the rules…"

"Ah! Spoken like a truly creative person, Lily. Well, it's a good idea." Grandmaman smiles.

"Thanks, Grandmaman. I also have lots of really super-cool ideas for my birthday ballgown…"

My mother clears her throat and calls her lady-in-waiting on duty – Madame Lejeune – to ask her to take a few pictures of me to show people. "Lily, why don't you go into the garden with Madame Lejeune – the light is better out there for photos. Then come back in for a quick bite to eat."

Coco follows me out of the dining room and downstairs to the drawing room that looks out onto the garden. As we make our way to the garden doors I grab a pair of pink sunglasses from the basket we keep on a chest of drawers. I put them on as I step onto the sunny upper terrace of the palace garden. Without giving it much thought I pluck a few of the season's last roses from the large planted border and place them in my hair – my dungarees are now a gardening uniform, after all! Then I do a few fun poses and Madame Lejeune takes some snaps. A few minutes later I rush back into the palace for a lightning-fast breakfast before heading to my bedroom to change into my school uniform.

I feel like I'm running on air as I speed through the palace. **"I GET TO DESIGN MY BIRTHDAY BALLGOWN!"** I yell to myself as I swing my rucksack over my shoulder and slide down the shiny brass handrail of the grand staircase. The palace cleaners attempt to curtsy to me, but I'm zooming past too quickly. Coco runs alongside me down the stairs, her bark echoing loudly against the marble walls. I land with a flying leap that sends Alice's eyebrows further up her forehead – she's waiting for me at the bottom of the stairs.

"I know, Alice – I shouldn't slide down the banisters but I'm so excited!!! Have you heard? I get to design my birthday ballgown!"

"I have, and that's lovely. The queen is going to show me some pictures of your gardening dungarees. I'm on my way to see her now. Don't forget your Princess Class tonight is in the—"

I don't listen to the rest of what Alice has to say, though, because I'm running late and I need to see Leonie before class starts. "I'll see you later, Alice!" I yell as I race out of the palace.

Leonie is waiting for me at the school gates. "And?" she asks.

"Yes! My mum and grandmother loved my idea for the new gardening uniforms, so I get to design my birthday ballgown!"

"**OMG!** That's fantastic!"

"I know!!! And have you seen how many views I've had on the Dreamy Dungarees video?"

"Masses! The video looks so good – especially the lighting."

"It's true. We make such a good team!" As Leonie

and I start walking to maths, I spot Max coming towards us down the corridor. Surprisingly, as he approaches he smiles.

Yes, **SMILES**.

He's not waving one of his #boysarepeopletoo posters or trying to push his gender-equality agenda on me. He smiles and tries to say something but the class bell rings just as he opens his mouth. Perfect timing, I think, because, to be honest, I feel like I've heard enough these last few weeks. Leonie and I keep moving and duck into the classroom as the bell dies down.

It's really hard to concentrate on learning about Waldenburgerish pronouns when visions of sparkly, colourful ballgowns are dancing through my mind on an endless loop. I have so many ideas that after a short while I've sketched masses of designs all up and down the margins of my notebook.

I hope that Frau Hauschka and her team will like my gardening uniform design as much as Mum does. And if I can also design a ballgown that impresses everyone, maybe Mum will start to take my fashion ambitions seriously. And then, if that happens, maybe I can vlog without having to keep Tiara Girl a secret...

Maybe?

I royally hope so!

12.17 p.m., in the school's auditorium

Normally I'd be in our school cafeteria right now but Leonie is rehearsing for the new school play in the auditorium and she asked me if I wanted to watch. I said yes because I always pay Leonie back for helping with my videos by helping her dress for her roles.

The Drama Club's next production is *Sleeping Beauty* – well, the Waldenburg version of it – and Leonie is playing the lead. In Waldenburg the roles of the prince and princess are different from what they are in the rest of the world. Here, in our matriarchal and matrilineal country, the roles have traditionally always been reversed, so the princess is the dragon-slaying warrior and the prince is asleep in a tower, waiting to be awakened by a kiss from the princess.

I know that Leonie is going to be a fantastic dragon-slaying princess. I mean, if I were a dragon I wouldn't even bother fighting with her because she has so much confidence she'd lay you flat quicker than the time it takes to put on a tiara. Speaking of which, I custom-made her a fabulous tiara for this role because the ones in the school costume department did not look authentic. I've also added some silver glitter **DIY** to her sword and shield. They look amazing!

Max has the role of the prince and he has put some of his #boysarepeopletoo posters up on the auditorium doors. When he sees me he makes a point of coming over and asking me why it is that in Waldenburg the boys are always passive, just waiting for a princess to come and save them.

I try to stay calm as I answer. "But, Max, in most other parts of the world it is the princess who is stuck in the passive, helpless, waiting-to-be-kissed-by-a-prince role. So I'm proud that Waldenburg offers girls a strong, alternative role model."

Max nods thoughtfully. "Look, I don't mind playing a passive prince – sometimes. But in Waldenburg the prince is *always* passive. Don't you think it would be cool to have an active prince sometimes, too?"

"I can't make that decision – it is something we must all decide together, don't you think?"

He's about to say something when he's called back onstage. "We'll discuss this more later – I look forward to it."

I don't say anything but unless he's planning to stop me in the school hallway – and I'm determined to avoid that happening – I can't see when.

I quietly pull out the copy of the speech I'll have to give at the animal rescue centre and silently read through it until Leonie appears onstage.

After rehearsal I wait for Leonie in the corridor. When she joins me, I notice she looks alarmed. "Have you seen it?" she asks as we head out through the nearest door and sit on a bench.

"Seen what?" She looks so worried. What could possibly have happened?

Leonie doesn't take her eyes off me as she hands me her phone. I peer at the screen and see that the Royal Court's official Instagram account has posted one of the pictures Mum's lady-in-waiting took of me this morning, in the garden – and it already has masses of Likes. But straight away I also understand why Leonie looks so alarmed: in the picture I look **VERY** similar to Tiara Girl in the Dreamy Dungarees video… maybe *too* similar. Just thinking about it gives me a queasy feeling and I can't help but wonder if anyone else has noticed the similarity. I royally hope not.

"Are you thinking what I'm thinking?" Leonie asks.

I nod and say, "But I thought the picture was just for Alice and a few others. I mean, no one mentioned anything about posting it on the palace's account – even if I've often asked to be on it! Then again, Mum did mention possibly posting a picture on social media – but I thought she meant the finished design – not the prototype!"

I take out my phone and find my Dreamy Dungarees video. Leonie and I start comparing both – and they are definitely, worryingly, alike. Even if in the picture I don't look *exactly* like I do in my video... still...anyone who watches my latest video and sees this post from the palace is bound to notice the striking similarities: green dungarees, colourful sunglasses, fun pose, flowers in my hair – although good thing I wear a wig in my videos!

HOLY ROYAL MELTDOWN!

What am I going to do?

I have thousands of followers on my Tiara Girl channel and the palace has hundreds of thousands of followers on their social media accounts. Surely there's a chance someone will put two and two together and realize that Tiara Girl and Princess Lily are the same person? And if they alert the press or the palace it'll all be over... I'll have to stop vlogging and I'll be thrown in the dungeons until I learn to be the perfect princess and give up vlogging!

How long before my cover is royally blown?

Days?

Hours?

Minutes?

I already have one anonymous fan who claims to know that I'm both Tiara Girl and Princess Lily – they left a letter in my school locker last week but so far they have kept it a secret. Who's to say others would do the same?

I feel sick…

"I think we have to face the fact that someone might recognize you," Leonie says. "Can you ask the palace to delete the picture?"

"I can…but that will make them suspicious because I'm always complaining that I want to be on social media and they've never let me before!"

"Then how about you delete your video?"

"That would also be weird. Especially because the video now has…" I look it up on my phone. "Seventeen thousand views." I stare at Leonie. "That's almost as many as my Top Five Tips for Wearing a Tiara video! Viewers would definitely ask questions if I deleted it now – so far it's my second most popular video ever! I'm stuck either way!"

Leonie nods. "What we need is a plan to deflect the attention from the palace post so that no one starts making the link between the royal you – Princess Lily – and the online you, Tiara Girl."

I'm in such shock I can only nod.

"We should meet after school…"

"We can work on a plan before my Princess Class tonight… **OMG!**" I clap my hands to my mouth because I've just remembered that I have my first waltz class later!

What a royal mess!

Chapter EIGHT

3.31 p.m., in my bedroom

"I probably should have thought more about what I was doing when I posed in the garden this morning," I say to Leonie. "But how was I to know that the palace would post the picture and that it would go viral?"

I'm looking at my phone. On the royal family's official Instagram account my photo now has 60,772 Likes. That's more than any other recent photo the palace has posted except for last week's #throwbackthursday photo showing my parents hosting their first official state visit as a married couple – something Sandra was pleased to point out to me when I met her just now, downstairs in the Marble Hall.

"You and your sense of style are very popular," she said. "You've always wanted to be on Instagram, Your Royal Highness. And now you are – and making a big splash for something you designed yourself. Isn't that wonderful?" Sandra was very happy for me so I had to go along with it and say that, yes, wasn't it incredible? Leonie smiled and nodded at Sandra as she stood beside me.

I know a princess isn't supposed to lie but what choice do I have?

If I was a princess in a storybook I'd probably be swallowed up by a giant troll for lying so much.

As soon as we finish our homework Leonie and I collapse on my giant beanbag and try to think of a plan to keep viewers from making the link between Princess Lily and Tiara Girl.

"I can't think of anything!" I finally say after what feels like a century of silence. "I don't have one single idea." Coco is licking my hand and clearly senses the anxiety I'm feeling.

"Me neither," Leonie says. "Apart from asking the palace to delete the picture…"

"Which would lead to too many questions…"

"Or deleting your Dreamy Dungarees vlog post…"

"Ditto."

A wave of unease rushes through me. "I wonder if anyone has already…" I spring to my laptop, open it and scroll through all the new comments on Tiara Girl while Leonie checks for new comments on the palace Instagram account.

I'm about to breathe a sigh of relief when one catches my eye. **OMG!!!**

"Leonie, listen to this: 'Tiara Girl, you should check out the Waldenburg Royal Family account on Instagram because it looks like Princess Lilian of Waldenburg could be your style sister! You definitely have the royal touch. Love your flower crown, btw! Please show us how to make one!'"

I can feel my hands start to sweat. This is **WAY TOO CLOSE** for comfort. "What can I do?"

"I don't know. There's one on the palace Instagram account, too: 'Hey Waldenburg Royal Family! So nice to see a fun pic of Princess Lily! Insta-followers, if you like this pic I can recommend you check out the Tiara Girl videos for more of this kind of fun princess style! #royalstyle #royalfan…'"

WHAT?!? This is **SO NOT** what I want to happen!

When Leonie sees my face she says, "I know what you're thinking. But we'll come up with something – promise. I wish there was some way we could delete the comment on the palace Instagram… Can you do it from your phone?"

I shake my head. "No. It's controlled by the palace."

Leonie comes over and from behind my shoulder silently reads the comment on my vlog. "Maybe you should answer them and say something funny about the similarity? That way you make it obvious to people who read the comment that Tiara Girl is **NOT** Princess Lily." After a moment she adds, "At least the comment is friendly. And from the way both comments are worded it doesn't seem to me that they've worked out the real connection between you and Tiara Girl. They would have said so if they had…"

I agree...but, still, this shows that I can't be too careful.

With Leonie's help I answer the comment made on my vlog:

Hi there! Thanks so much for your super-kind comment! Ha ha! I love that you think I have the "royal touch". I'll be sure to check out the Instagram account. And #staytuned because I have lots of exciting posts coming up soon – including one on how to make your own flower-power crown! Hearts and glitter,

Tiara Girl xx

"Perfect," Leonie says. She's quiet for a moment before she adds in a serious tone, "And from now on you can't give any viewer even the teeniest, tiniest suspicion that you are *both* Princess Lily and Tiara Girl."

"I totally agree – but what more can I do? I already wear a disguise when I vlog, and I never talk about

Tiara Girl to anyone but you – and I even film it in a secret turret!"

"I don't know – yet. But I'll think of something... In the meantime, I have another idea. How soon can you post a new video?"

"I was going to film one this weekend, after my visit to the animal rescue centre..."

"I think you should get one ready **ASAP**. The thing is, the more new videos you post..."

I suddenly understand what Leonie is thinking. "The sooner viewers will forget about me in my dungarees!"

Leonie nods. "Exactly!"

"That's brilliant, Leonie!"

"I know." Leonie is looking at her phone again. "I wish the palace would post some new pictures on their Instagram, too. That would help... How often do they post?"

I shake my head. "I don't know. It just depends on what's going on."

"Hmm." Leonie shrugs her shoulders. "Anyway, what's most important right now is that you get another video up – pronto! At least we can control what *your* viewers see."

Leonie is **SO** right.

At that moment there is a knock on my door. "Your Royal Highness?"

Sandra walks in carrying three garment bags. "Countess Vendelstein and I thought it would be a good idea to bring you a selection of dresses for your ribbon-cutting ceremony at the animal rescue centre, so that you have time to look them over and choose the one you'd like to wear. I'm sure you'll be pleased with what I've chosen."

I seriously doubt it – not that I say this to Sandra.

I jump up and help Sandra carry the garment bags to my walk-in wardrobe and we unzip them. Judging from the first dress Sandra takes out it seems I was right – they follow the Royal Rules to a tee.

"I hope you'll like them," Sandra says as she adjusts the bright yellow dress on the hanger. "Countess Vendelstein has said that you can choose whichever one of these three dresses you'd like to wear on Friday. We were inspired to find something more your style after the picture of you went viral. Countess Vendelstein felt it would be fair to let you express your style with more flair than usual..."

I'm amazed at what I'm hearing: *they want me to express my style?*

So maybe something good came out of that palace post after all?

Although if this is what they think my style is, then I'm not quite sure what difference it has made...

"For instance," Sandra continues, "I thought you'd like this detail." She is pointing to the thin black belt around the waist of the yellow dress. "Normally I'd have accessorized this with a matching yellow belt, but knowing how you like contrast, I found a black one instead." Sandra clearly thinks she's being daring and excitedly smiles at me before pointing to a simply cut, light blue dress. "And I had the hem on this dress taken up to give it a younger feel."

Even hanging, I can tell that the dress's hem will

still fall at my knees – not above them. I can't imagine how long it was before! And *this* is Alice's idea of expressing my style?

Sandra's phone rings and she says, "I'm needed downstairs." Then, quickly pointing to the last dress – a pink one hanging behind the others, "That one is particularly pretty and I think it will suit you."

As we walk out of my wardrobe Sandra smiles at me before turning to leave. "I am also to tell you from Countess Vendelstein that you should wear a dress for your waltz lesson – one that's easy to move around in."

I watch Leonie put her hand over her mouth and try not to laugh out loud.

"I'm sure you'll have a lovely time. And tomorrow we can pick out the accessories for whichever dress you choose."

After Sandra leaves, Leonie and I lay all three dresses on my bed. Neither of us is drawn to the yellow or blue dress.

"But the pink one is really pretty," Leonie says. "And totally your style!"

I pick it up and after having a closer look at it, I'm happily surprised: it's light pink and has a tutu-style skirt. It's actually something I *might* design myself – maybe with a patch or two and some more glittery embellishment.

I quickly change into it. It has long sleeves with a slight bell shape at the wrists, a fitted bodice and a skirt that flutters just above my knees. It even has some glittery embroidery. **LOVE!**

I shake my hair loose and put on my round pink sunglasses before strutting back and forth across my bedroom. "What do you think?" I ask Leonie.

She is standing with her arms crossed, her head tilted at an angle as she inspects me through narrowed eyes. "I think it's great – it even looks like something you'd wear on your vlog…"

"I know, right? That's why I love it. It's the one I'm going to choose. I can't believe Alice okayed it."

But Leonie has a faraway look in her eyes. She is silent as she turns her attention from me to the other two dresses.

"**OMG!**" she says as she looks at me, eyes wide. "I have a plan – *the* plan! I know *exactly* what else we need to do to stop people from making a link between your two identities…but you won't be able to wear that dress…"

I frown at her, a little confused.

"It is gorgeous, no doubt. But it looks totally like something that you might wear on Tiara Girl, right?"

I nod. "That's why I like it."

"Exactly: *it's your Tiara Girl style*. But I think that from now on you have to develop a stronger *Princess Lily style* – especially when you are carrying out public royal duties. And it should be a royal style that is completely different to your vlogging style."

I'm more confused now, because Leonie sounds exactly like Alice did on Monday at Princess Class when she told me that I have to develop a princess style for royal duties…

"But why can't I just happen to like this kind of style – even if I am a princess? I mean, I could name a few stylish princesses who don't always wear princess-perfect dresses."

"I'm sure you're right – *but do any of them have a secret fashion vlog?*" She shakes her head so hard her curls shake. "You, however, do." Leonie starts pacing my bedroom. "I mean, think about it: the bigger the difference between the two Lilys, the lower the risk that people will suspect that you are both! Trust me, I know – I'm an actor. I know what movie stars have to do to keep their private life private."

"But I'm not a movie star."

"True…but you are someone with a public persona – two of them, in fact. So that's kind of like being a movie star. Look, Lily, the point is: your Tiara Girl followers are increasing, right?"

I nod.

"And so are your royal duties… Taken together that means that more and more people, both in real life and online, will see you on TV, in newspapers… But if Princess Lily looks totally different from Tiara Girl, nobody will guess your secret."

"Hmm…" I'm starting to understand Leonie's point – even if I don't like it. After all, it means doing *exactly* what my parents and the palace want me to do.

Will I ever be able to do what *I* want?

"Do you see what I mean?" Leonie faces me with her hands on her hips. "Here, I'll show you." She takes her camera out and takes a quick picture of me dressed as I am and making a typical Tiara-Girl-style pose.

Then she walks to my bed and picks up the pale blue super-classic princess-style dress. It has absolutely no embellishment at all – except for a very thin and very simple matching bow at its waist. "I suggest that you wear this one on Friday." She holds the dress up in front of her. "No one will possibly guess that you are Tiara Girl. I mean, it's **SO** not your style."

I put it on so we can have a look, then Leonie motions for me to follow her to my bathroom. There she sits me down on a chair and brushes my hair until it's shiny and smooth. Then she slips a discreet dark blue velvet headband onto my head and together we choose a simple gold chain with a small heart pendant on it and a pair of dark blue patent-leather ballet pumps and matching blue coat.

I look at myself in my full-length mirror and have to admit Leonie has a point. If only Alice could see me now – she'd love it! Dressed and styled like this I totally look like a perfect princess – and nothing like the online Tiara Girl Lily! It would be *impossible* for anyone to guess that I'm the designer and stylist behind the glittery, colourful creations on Tiara Girl...

"I think your idea is brilliant, Leonie!" I say with a laugh. "Even if I don't like doing it." I'm quiet for a moment. "I'll post another Tiara Girl video tomorrow – I have a couple of ideas for themes – but what about the palace Instagram post? That's still online... What if someone asks me about it at the animal rescue centre?"

"Just say it's a funny coincidence. But we have to be more careful from now on. By dressing like a princess when you're doing your princess stuff..."

"And by dressing like my true self when I'm Tiara Girl..."

We decide to code name it our **Perfect Princess Plan**.

So much for being a royal rebel – it seems I'm destined to be the perfect princess no matter what I do...although as long as I have Tiara Girl I guess I'm still a *secret* royal rebel! Leonie and I grab hands and dance for a moment.

But then she suddenly goes quiet. "Hmm...there's one more thing I've just thought of... Remember when we dressed as mermaids for the school talent show?"

I have no idea what she's getting at. "Yeah..."

"Where are the wigs – those green ones? Do you still have yours?"

I look in the cupboard where I keep all of my old costumes. I find it at the bottom of the drawer and put it on my head. "It's a bit short," I say as I walk back out into my bedroom. My hair pokes out from underneath it.

"That doesn't matter – we can tuck your hair in. It's perfect!" Leonie says as she takes a brush from my dressing table and starts styling it. The wig is bright green and chin length so it's quite a bit shorter than the long pink vampire wig I've used in my videos so far. "You should wear this when you film your next few vlogs...and then change it for another wig in a few weeks."

"Is this part of the **Perfect Princess Plan**?"

Leonie nods. "It'll help keep people guessing what you really look like. This hair is shorter than your pink wig – and that's good. People won't know if you really have short hair or long hair."

The more I think about it, the more I'm sure this new plan can work. It's worth a try, anyway.

"Do you think I can pull it off?" I ask. The thought of telling Alice that I'd like to wear the pale blue dress to my first solo royal appearance is freaking me out. "I mean, what will Alice think when I go to her and say, 'Oh, by the way, Alice, I've chosen *not* to wear the super-cool pink dress you chose because actually I really feel like wearing a super-classic princess dress?' She's never going to believe me!"

"You're going to have to make her believe you!" Leonie jumps up again. "Just get into it! Be a princess who makes her own decisions!"

Leonie is right. I always complain that in fairy tales in the rest of the world the princesses are so passive and just kind of waiting around for stuff to happen. Now is my chance to prove that some princesses have plans of their own!

"I'll do it!"

"Yes!"

Then Leonie and I do a double high-five and start to dance again.

Coco sits in front of me and barks loudly.

"What does she want?" Leonie asks.

"**OMG!** Princess Class!" It's 5.45 p.m. and I have to be in the ballroom in fifteen minutes!

"How does she know what time it is?" Leonie asks as I dash to my wardrobe.

"Because she's royally clever!" I say as I take the pale blue dress off to keep it clean for Friday. I reach for the yellow dress that Sandra brought and quickly put it on. Then I exchange my blue velvet headband for a black one. "Is this princessy enough?"

"It's exactly what a perfect-princess-trying-to-hide-her-identity-as-a-secret-vlogger would wear."

I twirl in the dress and watch as the skirt flares. It's kind of boring – at least *I* think so. But it's perfect for Princess Class tonight.

I remember one thing before I leave my room: a pair of Doc Martens.

"Those, on the other hand, are not very princessy," Leonie says.

"True, but I bet my partner will have dance moves as clumsy as a dinosaur's."

"Good point."

Leonie gathers up her things and I show her out, with a promise to message her straight after Princess Class. I wish she could stay but she has to be home to babysit her younger brother.

Chapter **NINE**

6.00 p.m., Princess Class in the ballroom

I push open the large double doors and run towards the centre of the double-height ballroom. The enormous crystal chandeliers are ablaze with light and reflected hundreds of times in the large mirrors that line the walls. Towering gold candelabra are lit with real candles, their soft light flickering in the vast space.

I can make out Alice's shiny white hair and Grandmaman's elegant silhouette. But what I see next nearly causes me to smash into the chairs set up near the middle of the ballroom.

It's **MAX!!!** He's talking to Grandmaman and Alice

– and another older woman. She must be the dance instructor. But why is Max here? Surely he hasn't come to try and talk to me about equality? It's bad enough I have to see him at school – now he's even in my home! **WHAT IS HE DOING HERE?**

I don't have the chance to ask because Alice comes towards me. "Princess Lily, that yellow colour suits you so well." She clearly loves my dress. Although I see her purse her lips slightly as she takes in my shoes. "Perfect timing: your dance partner has just arrived." Before I can respond Grandmaman steps towards me and says, "Lily, I hardly need introduce you to Max. I'm sure the two of you will make wonderful dance partners."

SERIOUSLY?

Surely he can't be my dance partner? Alice knows I had a huge bust-up with him a few days ago! Plus, Grandmaman knows that Max and his #boysarepeopletoo group followed me all around school last week, chanting my name and waving signs in their quest to get my attention.

"Max, is the USA Under-21 Waltz Champion,"

Alice adds. "We are lucky he lives in Waldenburg and is available to help us out."

LUCKY?!?

"And meet Madame Dhutot your teacher," Grandmaman says.

I'm in such shock that I feel frozen to the marble floor. I can barely extend my hand and smile and say hello to Madame Dhutot. And I know it's rude but I can't bring myself to say anything to Max, who is waiting next to her. I turn to Grandmaman and hiss through gritted teeth, "Can I please speak with you, Grandmaman? Now?"

"Of course," she says softly. "But say hello first." Grandmaman is not amused, I can see that. Princess Rule Number 1 is to **ALWAYS BE POLITE**.

I take a breath and turn to Max.

"Thanks for inviting me, Lily," he says. "I'm excited that we'll have some time together and hopefully discuss gender equality – and that I'm able to help you out."

Gender equality?

Help *me* out!?!

I can practically feel the smoke come out of my nostrils in the most un-princess-like way. Alice clears her throat with a short, sharp cough and I can sense her glaring at me. I somehow manage to extend my hand and say hello to Max and before I turn to Grandmaman and we walk to the side of the room so we can't be overheard.

"Lily, what is the meaning of this? And why were you so rude just now to poor Max?"

"Grandmaman, why is Max my partner? You know what happened last week… I can't—"

Grandmaman holds up one of her bejewelled hands. "It was Madame Dhutot who proposed Max as your dance partner – and Alice, your mother and I agreed."

"You agreed?"

Grandmaman nods.

"But **WHY?** You know he was following me all over school last week and keeps pestering me about everything he wants me to change when I become queen!"

"That's precisely why we agreed. Lily, as a queen

you will have to deal with many different political factions here in Waldenburg – and regardless of any differences of opinion, you must listen to them and find a way to work with them. With Max as your dance partner, you will not only learn to waltz, but you will begin to learn the art of diplomacy. In fact, this is a doubly important Princess Class for you."

I COULD CRY!!! "But I don't like him! How am I supposed to dance with someone I don't like?"

"Do you remember the state visit your mother hosted last year? For that horrid dictator from that country – the name of which we shall not mention?"

I nod.

"As queen you will sometimes have to deal with people you don't particularly like or agree with. It is a part of our job, I'm afraid, Lily. So you'd better start getting used to it. Max seems a very nice boy, by the way. I've also met his parents recently. His mother sits on the boards of several large companies and his father is American. They've recently moved back after a few years in the US. Just be friendly and listen to him, Lily. The worst thing you can do as a future queen is to ignore a fellow Waldenburg citizen."

"But—"

"There will be no buts, Lily," Grandmaman says. "I have to go and Madame Dhutot is waiting. Don't worry – everything will be fine. Think of your birthday ball – and the dress you will design for it!" She gives me a smile before she turns and leaves.

THREE THINGS ALICE SAYS EVERY PRINCESS SHOULD KNOW ABOUT WALTZING IN WALDENBURG:

1. In other countries a gentleman asks a queen to dance...but not in Waldenburg. Here, tradition dictates that the queen asks her chosen gentleman for a dance. "Great!" I whisper to Alice while Madame Dhutot and Max discuss a dance step. "In that case Max need not come again because I did not, and will not, ask him to dance!" But Alice crisply answers that waltz lessons don't count.

2. A Waldenburg queen always opens the ball

(because she is the hostess) and dances the first dance with her husband, and the second dance with the next highest-ranking male guest, which will often be the head of state of another country, and so on. At my birthday ball, however, I will open the ball by dancing the first dance with my father. Thereafter I must dance with all the other male heads of state present. "Maybe they'll all get food poisoning and I won't have to ask anyone to dance," I say to Alice. She purses her lips before answering, "That's not the sort of thing a princess says. Besides, Princess Lily, my husband is never sick and he would love to dance with you." The thought of dancing with the truly ancient Count of Vendelstein instantly silences me.

3. When a queen of Waldenburg approaches her chosen dance partner, she must make direct eye contact with him and bow her head (basically, touch her chin to her chest) as a signal that she would like to dance with him,

at which point the chosen gentleman must bow deeply (bend from the waist) to the queen as a sign of acceptance. **FYI**: this is proof that when you are a princess you have to follow Royal Rules even when you're dancing!

Madame Dhutot is teaching us the "Waldenburg Waltz", which begins with a brisk tempo and full spin and dip to the right before settling into a more traditional rhythm. I grit my teeth and try to smile as Max and I place our hands on each other's shoulders and start to shuffle across the marble floor.

This is **SO NOT** like in the movies, by the way, where dance scenes are usually kind of dreamy!!! I've never waltzed and Max is clearly having trouble learning to follow – not lead. He almost steps on my toes a couple of times.

As my feet respond to the beat of the music, I try my best to concentrate on the new dance steps Madame Dhutot is teaching us. Her raspy voice is completely at odds with the romantic tones of the waltz music. And she is circling us, inspecting our every dance step with her beady eagle eyes, which is very distracting.

At first Max is too busy concentrating to say anything. I know he has a lot he wants to talk to me about, though, because I notice a wad of paper with a list written on it sticking out of his pocket. At the top of the list is my name alongside #boysarepeopletoo. Later, after we're moving more smoothly, he starts to say something a couple of times, but is cut off by Madame Dhutot clapping her large, bony hands and screeching, *"Un, deux, trois! Un, deux, trois!"* to the beats of the waltz.

At one point Madame Dhutot notices Max trying to say something and she rushes up to us. "Concentrate! Concentrate!" she yells above the music. Then she nearly karate-chops Max as she claps her hands together just beside his ear. The gold bangles on her wrist bang together with a clash that echoes around the ballroom. Ha! I'm almost starting to enjoy this!

If Madame Dhutot continues her loud clapping and counting at every dance lesson then these waltz classes will be much easier than I thought because

Max won't be able to get a word in.

PHEW!

As we reach the end of our lesson Madame Dhutot asks Max and me to stand facing each other in the centre of the ballroom. She wants us – or more precisely, me – to practise asking a gentleman to dance. Needless to say I would **NEVER** in a **MILLION YEARS** ask Max to dance.

"Step gracefully towards your chosen gentleman, Princess Lilian, please!" Madame Dhutot instructs. "Max, pay attention to her – pretend you've noticed the Princess looking at you from across the crowded ballroom." Max actually blushes when Madame Dhutot says this. I pretend I don't notice.

"The Princess is now gracefully moving towards you, Max. As she approaches she makes eye contact – *the princess makes eye contact!*" Madame Dhutot's voice goes up an octave as Max turns an even brighter shade of red and I try to look at him like I actually want to dance with him. *"Voilà!* And now bow, Princess Lily, **BOW**! And you now, Max, **BOW**!" I feel totally flustered by the instructions because I know we shouldn't bow at the same time but it all sounds like that's exactly what she's asking for! I'm confused about who she is talking to and it seems Max has bowed wrongly because she's yelling at him to try again.

"Bow again, now! Bow! **NOW!**" She's standing beside us and her hand movements aren't clearly directed, so I'm not sure if I should bow now or Max. Then she suddenly yells, "Princess Lily!" into my ear, startling me, and I bow, but too late I notice Max has also bowed and his head is coming up just as mine is going down.

That's the last thing I remember because suddenly everything goes totally dark.

The first lesson ended in Max and me headbutting each other. Both of us were so busy concentrating on Madame Dhutot's relentless orders that by the end neither of us understood whose command was whose.

Alice has called for ice packs and Max and I are sitting on one of the elegant ballroom sofas lined up against the walls. Alice decides against calling Dr Leclerc – apparently we are fine. After the initial burst of agony, the pain in my nose (thanks, Max) has settled into a kind of dull throbbing.

"The ice pack will help with the swelling," Alice says, "and your faces will be back to normal in no time."

Swelling?

What swelling?

Max and I wriggle around to get a look in the mirror on the wall behind us.

OMG!!! My nose is the size of a **SMALL PUMPKIN!!!**

What is it going to look like for my visit to the animal rescue centre?

And what about my Tiara Girl videos???

I KNEW WALTZ CLASS WAS A TERRIBLE IDEA!

"I'm sorry," Max says as we both look in the mirror. "I was listening to Madame Dhutot and—"

"It wasn't your fault, Max. I'm sorry, too…" I say as I catch his eye in the mirror. Max's forehead is just as bruised as my nose. At least when it comes to headbutting, Waldenburg is gender equal! Not that I say this to Max.

We turn back around to face Madame Dhutot, who is peering at us from behind her heavily mascaraed lashes. Clearly, the lesson did not end as she had hoped but she puts a good spin on things regardless. "I am very, very sorry about this. However I thought the lesson went well otherwise – I was very pleased with your dancing, Princess Lily. You have a good sense of movement. I feel you are a natural dancer."

Considering the fact that I need an ice pack on my face after my first ever lesson, I have a hard time believing this.

Alice starts making arrangements for next week. "Same time, same place," she says. While she finalizes the details with Madame Dhutot, Max pushes his gender-equality notes deeper into his pocket and mumbles something to me about next time. Then, one hand to the ice pack on his forehead, he turns to shake my hand and says goodbye.

And just like that, it's over.

Alice walks with me out of the ballroom and as we

do she hands me her phone. The screen shows my palace Instagram post and it now has 87,533 Likes!

That's **HUGE!**

I'm royally thrilled...as long as I don't think about the possible consequences for my Tiara Girl identity.

"Congratulations, Princess Lily – you must be proud. Your post is doing phenomenally well – and it's your first time on social media! Your idea for the gardeners' uniforms is clearly popular," Alice says as she takes her phone back. "And you always wanted to be on Instagram!" Alice is smiling and I can't let her know what I really think.

Instead I say, "Yes, it's been a real surprise."

"A happy one, I hope?"

"Oh yes," I say as enthusiastically as I can.

"Good. I am also very much looking forward to seeing which dress you choose for your visit to the animal rescue centre – although I have a strong feeling I know which one it will be." She half whispers, "I thought that pink one would really suit you."

I feel a pang of guilt for all of the fibs I'm telling Alice and I suddenly think that maybe I should tell her straight away that I've chosen the very formal and princessy blue one. But I can't. She is so excited for me and I know that she is really making an effort. Plus, knowing Alice, she's sure to be surprised if I *don't* choose the pink dress – and might start asking questions why. That could easily lead to trouble because if Alice (aka the human lie detector) doesn't feel I'm answering her truthfully she'll get suspicious... Why does life have to be so royally complicated? Instead I say, "They are gorgeous – and, yes, the pink one is just my style!"

I'll have to let her know about my choice of dress before our visit to the animal rescue centre...*but when? And how?*

And more pressingly, how am I supposed to film myself for Tiara Girl when my nose is bigger and redder than any ruby in the Crown Jewels?

Chapter TEN

7.30 p.m., in the small dining room

I end up having dinner with Dad. And Coco, of course – although she's already eaten so she just curls up at my feet and snoozes under the table with her head on my foot.

"How did your waltz lesson go?" Dad asks. "I mean, apart from you know…" He glances at my nose.

It's still swollen, although the pain has subsided. "I guess it went well, considering how it ended…"

"Madame Dhutot is the one who taught your mum and me to waltz. And once, in order to teach me a particular step, she took over from Mum."

"You had to dance with her?"

Dad nods as he slices the venison steak on his plate. "I kept getting my steps wrong, which meant the point of her shoe would accidentally kick me in the shin. She also squeezed my shoulder so hard I had to stretch it out after the class! She might not appear strong – but my goodness, she is." Then Dad asks, "Are you ready for your ribbon-cutting on Friday?"

"I think so... Alice has given me my speech – but it's only a few paragraphs long, so I've already memorized it."

"Good. And what about your outfit? Is it sorted?"

"Umm...yes, actually, it is." Which is true – thanks to my new plan. Not that Dad can know anything about it...

"And I've heard Alice will be accompanying you?"

I nod, then after a moment I ask, "Dad, do you think there is a chance the scissors might slip from my hands just as I'm about to cut the ribbon? Or that I'll forget my speech? I mean, I couldn't even get through my first waltz class without, you know..." I point to my nose. "It seems to me that all sorts of things could go wrong – and there'll be a ton of people watching!

Even the television stations will be there to film me for the evening news!"

Dad smiles. "Don't worry. Everything will be fine – that's what Alice is there for." Then he leans across the table and says, "But here's my Royal Tip of the Day, Lily: if something does not go according to plan, just smile, stay calm and carry on as if nothing has happened. Remember: everyone turns out to see *you* – not the ribbon being cut. As long as you take a genuine interest in the proceedings, the rest will be forgotten. That's what I've learned, anyway, since marrying your mother."

"Thanks, Dad."

I sure hope he's right because I don't want to go down in the history books as Lily the Clumsy just because I struggled to cut a ribbon or stumbled through my speech – or finished my first waltz class with a swollen nose.

Then again, how about my much bigger problem? What am I supposed to do if a journalist (Alice says the palace is expecting about a hundred or more) stands up in front of the crowd and shouts, "Hey!

Princess Lily, you're Tiara Girl, aren't you?"

There's no Royal Tip of the Day to help with *that* scenario…

To keep myself calm, I remind myself of…

MY THREE-POINT PERFECT PRINCESS PLAN:

1. Dress like the perfect princess whenever I'm on royal duty. A good choice would be: a simple dress, no pattern, pastel colour, ballet pumps. Thinking about this gives me the royal zzzzs, but what can I do?

2. Remember: there might be a Tiara Girl follower standing in the crowd! Therefore, do not wear colourful sunglasses or pose in any way that could remind anyone of my secret online persona.

3. Do not use phrases that I use on my vlog like, "Have a glittery week!" or "**LOVE!**"

Before I go to bed I finish the emerald tiara I've been

making for Zoë. **FYI**: the emeralds and diamonds aren't actually real – I use crystals that are made here in Waldenburg. I try it on her before I put her back in her cage and she looks **SO CUTE** in it! She seems to like it – her nose is twitching a lot, which is a sign that she's interested. Also, I think the colour combination of the emeralds and diamonds works really well with her brown and white coat.

Then, while I make a few last minor adjustments to Zoë's tiara, the **PERFECT** idea comes to me: my next Tiara Girl vlog post should be *all green*. I could feature Zoë's emerald tiara and how I made it! And in the video I will wear my green wig for the first time, which will look totally awesome because it will match Zoë's tiara! And I wanted to include Cupcake again and this could be perfect because her palomino colouring looks gorgeous in green. I could make her a green tiara, too! I even have a foam-green tulle skirt that I can customize with glitter – the same glitter I'll spray on my green wig! And maybe I can snip a tiny bit of tulle from one of the under layers of my skirt and make Zoë a matching tutu! **OMG!!!** I'll call it **Tiara Girl's Top Tips for a Complete Glittery Green Look**. And I'll film it tomorrow after school!

I'm not sure how I'll manage to film Cupcake because I'll have to do it outside or in the stables and I might be asked too many questions… Or maybe I'll just take a quick photo of her wearing her tiara? Maybe a close-up of both of us wearing tiaras?

Hopefully my nose will be back to normal by then. I dash to my mirror to check and I swear it's less swollen.

YES!!!

I'm so excited that I jump onto my bed and start shouting, "I love vlogging! I love vlogging!" Coco jumps up onto my bed, too, and we're both bouncing up and down when I hear a knock at my door.

Grandmaman walks in and she's wearing a huge pearl and diamond tiara, a necklace of very large round pearls, plus a three-strand pearl necklace with a drop-shaped pearl pendant the size of a grape. A black pearl, surrounded by diamonds, sparkles at each ear. "What is it you love, Lily?"

I'm caught totally by surprise but luckily I stop myself before I answer, "Vlogging!" Even though I'm not sure Grandmaman knows what that means, why take the risk? Instead I say, "I love jumping."

"Oh…that's funny. It's not what it sounded like at all to me. I hope my hearing isn't starting to go," Grandmaman says.

I leap off my bed. "I'm sure it isn't, Grandmaman…"

Fortunately at that moment Grandmaman spies Zoë and the subject is changed. "What is that on her head?" she asks as I pick up Zoë.

"It's a tiara I made for her."

"It looks like one of mine," Grandmaman says as she peers at it closely.

"That's because I was inspired by the one you wore to the ambassadorial dinner last week."

"Yes, I see… You're so creative, Lily."

I say nothing but stare at Grandmaman and wait for her to continue.

"Speaking of which, I have some good news: a prototype of the gardeners' uniform will be ready tomorrow. If you approve it, a graphic artist will begin working to refine your idea for the coat of arms. You'll also be asked to look at fabric samples. Nothing will be finalized unless you've seen it. We've also found zip samples for the wonderful pockets you designed."

"That's so exciting, Grandmaman!"

"It is, I agree... In the end designing the gardeners' uniforms wasn't so difficult, was it, Lily?"

"It's just I was frustrated at the beginning because—" I suddenly stop because Grandmaman might not understand what I want to say and I don't mean to upset her.

"Yes, Lily?"

I take a breath and blurt out, "Because of all the rules."

"Ah, yes, the Royal Rules..."

I look at Grandmaman, my eyes wide. "Do you call them that, too?"

She nods and laughs. "I did when I was your age... But as you've shown us to great effect, you can work *with* them, can't you?"

I nod.

"By the way, I heard from Alice that she and

Sandra chose some very pretty dresses for your visit to the animal rescue centre. She mentioned a pink one in particular that is completely your style."

"Uh…yes, yes, it's very pretty."

"Good, Lily. I'm very happy for you. I'm sure you'll look lovely."

My smile is still frozen on my face. "I hope so."

As Grandmaman leaves my bedroom I wonder what will happen when they all find out that I am going to wear the one dress that is so totally **NOT** my style?

I can sense a royal inquisition ahead!

Chapter ELEVEN

7.03 a.m., Thursday, in my secret turret

I wake up extra early so I can prepare Cupcake's tiara and my green wig and tulle skirt for the video I want to film after school – and to check my nose, which looks more or less normal again **(PHEW!!!)**. Before I fell asleep last night I decided it would be best to prepare everything in my secret turret because I want to spray glitter all over my wig and skirt. Not only would the glitter spray make a **HUGE** shimmery mess in my bedroom, but I'd have to leave my skirt and wig out to dry and Sandra might see them when she goes into my bedroom to sort my clothes. She'd be bound to ask me what they were for.

In my turret I take my gorgeous green tulle skirt out of my rucksack and carefully place it on the mannequin I keep in a corner. Royal Confession: it's not a real mannequin like the kind you find at a dressmaker's – it's a super-simple one I made. I cut some white cotton fabric into a torso, two arms and two legs, sewed them together and stuffed them with old rags. But before stitching it together at the neck, and instead of adding a head (too complicated!), I slid an old wooden clothes hanger into the dummy, as shoulders, with the hook coming out of its "neck". It is floppy – no doubt. But, still, the padding helps me see the outfit better.

Before I forget I snip two pieces of tulle fabric from an under layer of the green tulle skirt and place them on my desk. I'll use them later to make Cupcake's tiara and Zoë's matching tutu.

I set my old mermaid wig on top of a shoebox that I've stood on its end on top of some old magazine pages I've ripped out and spread on the floor. Then I shake the cans of green, aqua and gold glitter spray, and start spraying the green one over my wig and skirt. I don't go in too close. I want the glitter to settle on the skirt and wig as lightly as possible – and just on the surface, so the hair and layers of the skirt won't be weighed down. I alternate spraying with the different colours, layering them together in some places and in others just leaving a light coating of one colour. When I'm finished I stand back to have a look. The glitter looks **SO COOL!** Like turquoise seawater that has flecks of gold swirling in it.

LOVE!

I leave my wig and skirt to dry while I cut and shape the thick wire for the base of Cupcake's tiara. I also cut some thin wire I've brought into long lengths. Next I wrap the long narrow piece of tulle fabric around the base, twisting it so it almost looks braided. After I secure both ends by binding the lengths of thin wire tightly around the fabric, I set the base down on some fresh newspaper and shake the glitter cans. Then I repeat the same spray-painting technique I used on my wig and skirt.

Afterwards I take out the small bag of crystals.

With my special glue (from Dickel's Hardware Shop) I carefully attach green, round crystals of various sizes all over the tiara base. The glitter spray paint isn't completely dry, obviously, but I don't have time to wait before applying the crystals.

I step back and admire my work. The tiara looks gorgeous and sparkly and it's bound to look amazing on Cupcake!

I check my wig and skirt again quickly before leaving it all to dry. Then I carefully turn the large gold key in the lock and head down the long spiral stone staircase, Coco at my heels.

Later on at school, Leonie and I walk together to my locker because I have forgotten my verb conjugation book. But when I open my locker I see a letter has been slipped through the door.

"It's another anonymous letter," I whisper to Leonie as I pick it up and turn it over in my hands. "I'm sure of it – it looks exactly like the last one. Same kind of envelope and handwriting."

"Open it," Leonie whispers.

We glance around us and although the wide corridor is busy with students, everyone is distracted. I quickly tear the envelope open.

Hi Lily,
This is a friendly letter just saying that I think you need to be more careful...
The picture the palace posted of you in the garden with your gardeners' dungaree design is great...but it looks an awful lot like your latest Tiara Girl post!
   Don't worry, though – your secret is safe with me.
   From,
   A fan

I try to stay calm as I read the letter.

"You were right," Leonie says. "It seems like it's been written by the same person, doesn't it?" I nod. "It's the same handwriting and the wording – *your secret is safe with me* – is exactly how the first letter ended, too. The first one is also signed: *from a fan...*"

"Yet we're no closer to knowing who it is."

I shake my head as I turn around and look up and down the corridor. "It could be anyone."

"I still think it's Max," Leonie says. "After all, he's on a mission to get your attention..."

"Yeah, but he sees me here at school – and now he has weekly waltz classes with me, too. He has plenty of opportunity to get my attention!"

"True. But he doesn't have time to talk to you here and you said that he didn't have a chance to get a word in during your dance class, either. Maybe he thinks this is the best way?"

"Maybe...but then you'd think he'd leave me letters about the issues he wants to discuss. I mean, why write this? It has nothing to do with gender equality," I say as I put the letter into my rucksack. "I think it's someone else...but who?"

The bell rings – it's time to go to our next class.

"I don't know – but we'll find out. In the meantime, the most important thing is that you stick to our new plan. We can't have more people guessing that you and Tiara Girl are one and the same," Leonie whispers as we walk to Waldenburgerish Class.

I have to admit that receiving another anonymous letter has made me feel jumpy and I can't stop wondering who else in my school might know that I am both me *and* Tiara Girl...

I quickly check my vlog on my phone as Leonie and I walk into our classroom.

Hi Tiara Girl! And welcome to your channel!

Your most recent video:

<u>Tiara Girl's Top Tips for Designing Dreamy Dungarees</u> has had:

21,855 views

Holy royal macaroni and **OMG!** This is my second video to get over 20,000 views! I pump my fists into the air with excitement but quickly stop myself when

I remember that I'd better look at the comments and find out if anyone has guessed that I, Lily Waldenburg, am also Tiara Girl …

I read every new comment but don't find one asking if I'm Princess Lily – or even saying that the Princess Lily post on the palace's Instagram account looks like my Tiara Girl post…

PHEW!

Long may it last! I can't wait to get my next Glittery Green video up!

When school ends Leonie and I meet just outside the gates. She has to go to a family dinner at her aunt's house, in a mountain village about an hour away, so she can't come and help me film my next video. Plus, because I'll be at the animal rescue centre tomorrow, I won't see Leonie until Saturday, when she'll come to the palace and sleep over.

We hug each other and Leonie says, "I'll be sure to watch the evening news tomorrow night. And I'll keep all fingers and toes crossed so that your **Perfect Princess Plan** goes without a hitch. I wish I could be there to help you!"

4.17 p.m., in my secret turret

My green wig and tulle skirt look **AMAZING!!!** And so does Cupcake's mermaid-green tiara. The glitter has dried and I am thrilled with the results. The golden afternoon light streaming through the windows makes everything shimmer and shine and I can't wait to put them on. But first I take Zoë out of my rucksack and put her tiara on her. She looks **ADORABLE!!!**

I unpin the small piece of fabric I'll use for Zoë's tutu and I cut it, using the pattern I brought up with me. Then I thread some fine ribbon through the small end to make a waist. I slip it on Zoë until it reaches her middle then tie the ribbon so that the tutu will stay put without squeezing her – and ta-dah! – it's finished! It matches her tiara beautifully and she looks like a guinea pig princess! I can't wait to start filming!

After I put on my wig, skirt and top (a green T-shirt with a large gold glitter heart that I've drawn in the middle of it), I try on a couple of pairs of sunglasses and decide that my star-shaped gold glitter ones work best.

LOVE!!!

I'm especially excited about filming this video because green is my favourite colour after purple – it reminds me of the Waldenburg forests, and riding with Cupcake, and the lush lawns around the palace, and just sunny days outside, in general, I guess.

TIARA GIRL'S TOP TIPS FOR A COMPLETE GLITTERY GREEN LOOK:

* Choose a top or skirt in green or light yellow or even white – whatever you think will lend itself to a green glitter finish. Just remember that the lighter the colour, the more visible the finish will be.
* If you don't have a special workroom I suggest you hang the clothes up outside because glitter sprays can make a mess.
* You can find glitter sprays at most craft shops and some florists stock them, too – especially at

Christmas. Make sure to get cans of green, gold and silver. Using more colours than just green will give your **DIY** fashion more depth and magic!

* After shaking the cans well, start spraying! Use gentle movements and spray lightly – you don't want to weigh down the fabric or make the glitter gloop together. Remember you can always build up layers!

* Let your customized clothes dry completely before putting them on.

* Another fun tip for a more precise glittery effect is to customize your clothes with glitter pens. I think it looks especially pretty and magical to combine the two effects on the same outfit!

* This is a look that you can easily share with your pets. Use my Glittery Green Tips to customize your pony's halter, for example – or make a **CUTE** glittery bandana for your dog! Just make sure to shake off any loose glitter particles because you don't want it to irritate their skin!

I'm having so much fun filming this video! And I'm pleased I include the tip about turning this look into one that can be shared with pets because Zoë looks adorable and I can't wait to see Cupcake in her tiara later!

Filming ends up taking longer than planned and by the time I've finished I'm in a rush: I only have an hour before I have to be at my Princess Class – and I still have to take a picture of me and Cupcake in our matching look!

I quickly change out of my vlogging outfit and into my jeans. Then I put Cupcake's tiara and my skirt into my rucksack and make sure Zoë is in there too (it's so royally **CUTE** how she sits on top of my things with her head poking out). I call for Coco, and then rush out of the palace to the stables. It's a good time to go because it will be quiet; the horses won't be fed for another hour, so no one should be around to see me.

Cupcake whinnies softly as soon as she hears me – she always recognizes the sound of my footsteps. As quickly as I can I brush her mane and forelock. Because I don't have much time I'm going to do a

close-up of our faces. Cupcake very sweetly lowers her head while I place the tiara on it and adjust it so that it sits in her lush forelock, just in front of her ears. It looks so green and sparkly and awesome!

LOVE!

Then I pull my skirt on over my jeans, place my green wig over my hair, and check my make-up, I take my phone out and start filming us together, just having fun. I also briefly explain how I've made Cupcake's tiara so viewers can do the same at home. Then I kiss her and style her hair (on film) with a side part because that looks good, too. I stop with a shot of me, Zoë and Cupcake in the frame together. It looks royally **ADORABLE!!!**

I put my phone down and I hear footsteps.

"Hello? Who's there?"

OMG!!! It's Alice!

WHAT IS SHE DOING HERE?

She never comes to the stables – **SO WHY NOW???**

And why is she here when Princess Class starts in five minutes! Normally Alice would be in the palace getting everything ready for my lesson!

This is a royal nightmare – especially as I've just realized that I still have my wig on – and my tulle skirt!

I stand as quietly as I can while I start wiping off my make-up. Maybe she'll leave... I watch as she stops to listen, then turns and walks away.

I'm just about to let out a long breath when Coco barks.

"Princess Lily?" I hear her footsteps head back in my direction. What am I going to do?

"Princess Lilian? Is that you?" she asks as she walks towards me. I have no chance to slip my wig off or even hide the skirt. "Whatever are you doing dressed like that in *here*?" she asks when she reaches Cupcake's stall door and sweeps her eyes over me. She looks surprised – and for once I can't say I blame her.

I smile and try to look like it's **PERFECTLY NORMAL** for a princess to walk around the stables wearing a bright green wig and customized glitter outfit, accompanied by a pony wearing a tiara and a guinea pig in a tutu.

I say, "Oh, hi, Alice. Yes, it's me. I'm just rushing

to make Princess Class. I need to change first, though."

"In the stables?" She gives me her best human lie detector look as she waits for an answer. **WHAT AM I GOING TO DO?** If I don't give her a good answer she's bound to bring this up with Grandmaman or my parents. "Well, you know how I love to design and customize my clothes…" I look down at my green glitter skirt. "So I thought I might make something for Cupcake, too."

Alice's eyes narrow.

"You see, we match." I point to Cupcake's tiara. Alice rolls her eyes. "One day, Lily, you will have to spend your time on more serious matters."

"I know…but I can't help designing things—"

"Indeed. And you are good at it, as we have found out." She glances towards my outfit. "These creative spirits!" She sighs.

"Er, yes, absolutely." I nod and try to look relaxed – which is no easy task when you're telling the biggest royal lie in all of history. But as unbelievable as it sounds, **ALICE DOESN'T QUESTION ME** – clearly, now that the gardeners' uniforms have been given palace approval, I'm going to be allowed to be more creative. I quickly slip out of my skirt and fold it into my rucksack, pick up the bag, then step out of Cupcake's stall and shut the door behind me.

Alice is waiting for me. "I heard you'd come to the stables and I wanted to show you these," Alice suddenly says as she shakes out a green bundle she's holding. "It's the prototype of your dungaree design!"

Typical! I didn't tell anyone I was going to the stables, so Alice must have called security, who'd have followed me at a discreet distance.

I reach for the dungarees, holding them up in front of me and turning them this way and that. They look **SO COOL!** And pretty much exactly as I'd imagined. "Wow! Thank you for showing me." I finally smile a real smile.

The palace chose a thick, heavy cotton for the fabric – although the shade of green is still a little bit off. It's a weird but super-exciting feeling to hold a professionally made prototype of something I designed. This must be what it's like for real fashion designers when they put a collection together for a fashion show and finally see their designs being modelled on the runway.

"Obviously, the coat of arms will be further refined, but we wanted you to see this in case you have any more suggestions to make – we are all thrilled with how it looks! And by the way, keep them – they're not exactly your size, but I thought you might like to try them on after your Princess Class. Speaking of which, we'd better hurry – Professor Hustemeier is probably waiting."

Alice leaves me with the dungarees and tells me she'll let Professor Hustemeier know that I won't be long.

I take a deep breath as I listen to her footsteps fade away. Then I take my wig off and finish wiping off my make-up. I dash out of the stables and across the courtyard to the palace and race up to my bedroom to leave Zoë and my rucksack there.

Life is royally exciting and complicated at the same time!

As I cross the ballroom I take my phone out and have a quick look at the palace's Instagram account... My photo now has over 156,000 Likes! I check the comments but don't come across a single mention of Tiara Girl.

PHEW!

Chapter TWELVE

6.17 p.m., in Grandmaman's sitting room

Professor Hustemeier is wearing one of her retro outfits – her clothes always look retro, but I don't think it's on purpose. She's wearing a rust-coloured trouser suit with an orange shirt, accessorized with a scarf in autumnal tones and brown leather loafers. She usually wears her hair scraped back and always has large black glasses perched on her nose. They'd make her look like an owl if she wasn't so tall. She's friendly but you don't want to get into a debate with her about Waldenburg history – she knows more about it than any other living person on the planet – cross my royal heart!

Today we discuss the details of my ribbon-cutting ceremony tomorrow and Professor Hustemeier talks to me about the history behind the royal walkabout – like, how my great-grandmother, Queen Lilian III, started the tradition so that people could actually see her up close, and maybe even meet her. Up to that point Waldenburgers would only ever have caught a fleeting glimpse of my family zooming past in their carriages, or if they were lucky enough to be invited to the palace for a ball. But my great-grandmother changed all of that – she made the royal family more *accessible*, as Professor Hustemeier puts it – and people loved her for it.

I also learned that the Hairy Hounds and Happy Horses Animal Rescue Centre was founded by a mother-and-daughter team – Madeleine and Annika Ingold. They used to live in a house just outside of Waldenburg town, on the edge of the forest. Lots of people would dump their dogs and cats – and even horses! – in the forest when they'd tired of looking after them. Annika and her mother would find them and bring them home until their house and garden were bursting with animals. That's why they've relocated to the larger premises I'm going to open tomorrow.

Finally I practise my speech a few times in front of Alice and Professor Hustemeier. Professor Hustemeier tells me it's good that I've memorized it because that means that instead of looking at my notes I can make eye contact with the audience.

"This is important for building a *rapport* with your audience," Alice adds.

I have no idea what she means but Professor Hustemeier clarifies. "People in an audience love eye contact, Princess Lily, so the more you can look at them the more it appears you are sharing a conversation with them and not just speaking *at* them." At least I understand THAT.

Professor Hustemeier shows me how to stand and breathe so I can project my voice – although there will, of course, be a microphone for me to use. She also explains that in front of the podium a small box will be placed for me to stand on. "It will give you added height so your voice will carry further and you'll be able to make eye contact with those at the back of the space." Professor Hustemeier stops to smile at me before saying, "I'm sure you'll be a success, Princess Lily."

I royally hope so! And I hope my **Perfect Princess Plan** will be successful, too!

Before Princess Class finishes for the night we go over tomorrow's programme one last time:

HRH The Crown Princess of Waldenburg

Programme for the opening of the

<u>Hairy Hounds and Happy Horses</u>

<u>Animal Rescue Centre</u>

8.30 a.m. Hair and make-up by Jacqueline. To be applied in the French Morning Room in the Renaissance Wing.

9.05 a.m. Departure from the inner courtyard, with the Countess of Vendelstein. Driver: Officer Heinz-Walther Werther.

9.27 a.m. Arrival at Tannenspitz, the village home of the animal rescue centre.

9.30 a.m. Escorted by palace police, the walkabout begins at the top of the high street, which will be closed for the occasion. The Countess of Vendelstein will act as lady-in-waiting.

10.00 a.m. Frau Theresa Müller (the mayor of Waldenburg town), Frau Laure Minette (mayor of the village of Tannenspitz), Frau Madeleine Ingold, her daughter Fräulein Annika Ingold and their staff will greet HRH The Crown Princess on the front steps of the animal rescue centre. Lilian, the foal named after HRH The Crown Princess, will also be present.

10.10 a.m. HRH The Crown Princess, Frau and Fräulein Ingold and the rescue centre staff will pose on the front steps of the rescue centre for an official photo opportunity for journalists.

10.17 a.m. The Mayor of Waldenburg will give her speech.

10.21 a.m. HRH The Crown Princess will give her speech.

10.25 a.m. HRH The Crown Princess will cut the ribbon.

10.30 a.m. HRH The Crown Princess will be escorted on a tour of the new premises and meet some of the rescue animals.

11.00 a.m. A second photo opportunity, inside the animal rescue centre, will be held for official journalists.

11.18 a.m. HRH The Crown Princess, accompanied by Countess Vendelstein, will depart.

11.40 a.m. HRH The Crown Princess will arrive at the palace.

When I say to Alice that it seems like an awful lot to pack into *one* morning Alice says that the life of a working princess is not all fun and games and that I'll have plenty of time to relax after I return from school.

"From school?" **WHAT?!?** I was sure I was having the day off!

Alice nods. "Yes. As you can see on your schedule you are busy only until 11.40, when we return to the palace. You will then change into your school uniform and eat a quick lunch here before you go to school for the rest of the afternoon."

GREAT!!! Everyone will have seen me on television in the morning and then I'll go back to school and be like, *Oh hey, it's just me. That's just my life now.* Which I guess it is, but, still, **HOW ROYALLY EMBARRASSING!!!**

Sandra is waiting for me when I step out of Princess Class. "Your Royal Highness," she says, "I thought I might help you accessorize your outfit for tomorrow before you have dinner."

OMG!!! I'd completely forgotten about Sandra!

"I'm sure you've chosen that lovely pink dress," she continues, "the one that is most your style. I know exactly which shoes and jewellery would look nice with it. You do not have to wear a hat and the queen has specified that your hair be worn loose and also that..." Sandra continues as we make our way to my bedroom. I don't know what to tell her – I don't want her looking at my outfit y*et.* She'll be surprised I want to wear the blue dress so I'd prefer to surprise her – and everyone else – with my choice tomorrow morning, when it's too late for too many questions... So what can I tell Sandra *right now* to get her off my tracks?

Suddenly, the perfect idea comes to me!

"Sandra, don't worry about anything because I am going to show my mother my outfit later tonight. She is going to help me put it together. I can't wait!"

Sandra sounds surprised and a little disappointed.

"You know how my mother is," I quickly add. "She's a perfectionist and this being my first solo royal duty and everything..."

"I understand, Princess Lily. And of course your mother will know what looks best for this special occasion. I will leave you here, then. But should you need any assistance please don't hesitate to call me. I will be here from 7 a.m. tomorrow morning. And if I may say so, Your Royal Highness, I very much look forward to seeing your dress choice then." Sandra smiles at me and I breathe a sigh of relief as she turns and leaves.

PHEW!

With so much to think about I'm not really in the mood to edit a video, but I do my best. A short while later I

press Upload. The timing couldn't be better, because tomorrow I'll be on every television channel as Princess Lily, appropriately dressed as the perfect princess. Viewers will have to be Sherlock Holmes to spot any resemblance between Princess Lily and Tiara Girl then.

Finally I get into bed and Coco straight away snuggles up next to me. I try to get some royal zzzzs but I keep thinking about tomorrow...

My hair and make-up will be done at 8.30 a.m. That means I'll have breakfast first – and then get dressed in my outfit. That's perfect because with any luck, I can get straight into the car and Alice won't notice a thing until I take my coat off at the animal rescue centre and it will be too late for her to question my choice!

I quickly call Leonie and tell her that she will see me at school tomorrow after all. "Yay! That's fabulous news!" she says.

"I'm happy I'll see you – but what about everyone else? I'll bet lots of them will have seen me on television. It's royally embarrassing!"

"You are the Crown Princess, you know," Leonie says. "There's not much you can do to change that so get used to it! More importantly, your new Tiara Girl video looks fab – and **SO** different from your last video. I think your viewers will be forgetting all about the dungarees already. And tomorrow, when you dress like Princess Lily—"

"No one will dream that we are the same person."

"Exactly."

Mum comes by to say goodnight just as I'm falling asleep. I can hear the rustling of her dress and smell her perfume as she walks in. "All set for tomorrow?" she asks.

I nod.

"And your outfit? Is it all laid out? Did Sandra help you?"

I'm suddenly very awake – even if I pretend not to be. I don't want **ANYONE** – even Mum – to see my choice of dress until the morning.

Instead I continue with the biggest lie in royal

history. "Yes, Mum, I discussed it with Sandra." Which I did, in a way… "I hope you'll like it."

"I'm sure I will. By the way, Frau Hauschka and the gardening team all love your idea for their uniform. We agreed this afternoon when we saw the prototype that we will definitely go ahead with your design. Isn't that exciting?"

I sit up. "Wow. That's great, Mum! I've already started sketching ideas for my ballgown!"

"That's a good idea, Lily, because we'll have to find the right dressmaker to sew your design and they will also need time to order the fabric. But first, you have to get through tomorrow. Sleep well and I'll see you in the morning."

Mum leans over and kisses me on my cheek.

I breathe a sigh of relief and snuggle up to Coco as Mum closes my bedroom door gently behind her. Then I do my best not to think any more about tomorrow…

Chapter THIRTEEN

7.03 a.m., Friday, at the palace

Hi Tiara Girl! And welcome to your channel!

Your most recent video:

<u>Tiara Girl's Top Tips for a Complete Glittery Green Look</u> has had:

2,557 views

YAY! I'm thrilled with how much my viewers seem to love it! And best of all, I've noticed that some of the comments are about my new wig, with viewers wondering what my real hair is like, which means that no one appears to have any idea about what I actually look like or who I really am!

PHEW!

It seems Leonie's plan is working!

Alice said last night that the palace will post some pictures on their Instagram account of me at the animal rescue centre. I'm pretty sure I'm safe now, but I'll have to be super careful **NOT** to repeat the mistake I made the other day. I cannot dress **ANYTHING** like Tiara Girl when I'm supposed to be Princess Lily...

Although I'm feeling too nervous to eat, I run down to the small dining room in my dressing gown. I have a quick breakfast and then run to meet Jacqueline in the French Morning Room. I've known Jacqueline since I was a child – she's been doing Grandmaman's hair and make-up since the olden days – so she knows exactly how I should look. Plus, Alice has briefed her – I spot the notes on the dressing table underneath a can of hairspray.

My hair will be loose, but blow-dried so it looks

smooth and has some bounce. And I won't wear much make-up – just some powder and blusher, a touch of mascara and a swipe of lip gloss. From what I can read of Alice's notes her instructions are very strict about how little make-up I should wear.

"You look *très jolie!*" Jacqueline smiles as she takes a last look at my reflection in the mirror.

Just then I smell roses and, sure enough, Grandmaman walks into the room. "Good morning, darling Lily. How do you feel? Not nervous, I hope?" Even though Grandmaman is wearing a dressing gown and pretty slippers, her hair and make-up look perfect and polished. And she has rings and earrings on. She always looks very regal – even first thing in the morning!

"I'm fine, Grandmaman," I say. And I guess I am – although I'll be really fine once this day is over!

At that moment Mum sweeps into the room. She is wearing her running kit and chunky sports watch. "I wanted to wish you good luck, Lily, before I have to dash off. I have meetings in Parliament later this morning and want to squeeze in a run before I go. But

I wish you a very happy day and a wonderful start to this new chapter in your life – your first solo royal duty is a big deal." Mum gives me a huge hug then turns to Grandmaman.

After a moment Grandmaman clears her throat and says, "You look lovely, by the way, Lily. Still thirteen – but like a Crown Princess about to begin her working life. Speaking of which...your mother and I want to give you something for good luck." Grandmaman reaches into the pocket of her dressing gown and pulls out a soft velvet pouch and hands it to me. "This is something I was given by my mother when I had my first solo royal engagement. I, in turn, gave it to your mother when she started..."

"And now I'd like to pass it on to you, darling," Mum says.

"We were both the same age as you when we received it."

I slowly and carefully open the pouch and pull out a small grey leather box. I press on the clasp and it opens to reveal a beautiful diamond brooch.

"It's in the form of a butterfly," Grandmaman

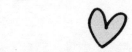

explains, "because your great-grandmother was given it as a gift from Waldenburg town when she opened the butterfly garden in the public park. That was her first royal engagement. She wore it often until she gave it to me."

"It's beautiful!" I say as I jump up, run to a mirror and hold it against my dressing gown. **I LOVE IT!!!** It's just like the butterflies on the patches of my dreamy dungarees. Only made of real diamonds. **HOLY ROYAL MACARONI!!!**

"I thought it would look nice on your dress today," Mum says. "Then again, it's so windy outside that you might wear it on your coat instead."

I give Mum and Grandmaman hugs and thank them. The brooch really is gorgeous!

After Grandmaman and Mum leave I say goodbye to Jacqueline then dash back to my bedroom to change. The pastel blue dress looks perfect. I put on a pair of nude tights (Alice always insists), navy patent-leather ballet pumps, and a lightweight princess-cut coat in a pretty light blue that is one tone darker than my dress. A small, round, navy patent-leather cross-body bag holds my lip gloss and phone. As for jewellery, I've chosen a delicate gold necklace with a tiny pearl pendant and matching tiny pearl earrings. A slim gold bracelet with my initials – and Coco, Zoë's, and Cupcake's, too – hanging from it in tiny gold letters completes my look.

Finally, I pin my butterfly brooch onto my coat and make sure to do up all of the coat buttons so that Alice doesn't suspect anything. But Sandra is probably on her way to check on me now and as she comes in her eyes widen as they sweep over me from head to toe. They stop at the bottom of my coat, where the hem of the pastel blue dress can be seen.

"Oh, you're in blue," she says, surprised. "I thought you'd choose the pink dress... It is so much more your style..."

"I know what you mean," I quickly answer. "But when I woke up and...and..." All of the excuses I've been thinking of rush through my mind – and not one sounds believable enough. I glance through the window and suddenly I know what to say. "When I woke up and saw the bright blue sky I thought it would be nice to match it. You know, for luck, so it stays sunny all day." I make sure to step close to Sandra so that she sees my new brooch. At the sight of it she forgets about my dress and instead checks to make sure that it is properly pinned and that its safety catch is closed.

Then she gets a call from Alice. "Countess Vendelstein is waiting for you in the inner courtyard, Princess Lily."

Before I dash out of my bedroom I make sure Zoë has fresh water and once I'm downstairs I kiss Coco goodbye and shake her paw for good luck. All the way to the car I go over my speech in my mind and try to breathe calmly. I walk slowly and with my back straight, like Alice always instructs me to do and tell myself I can do it, that I will be the perfect princess this morning – it's the only chance I have of keeping my vlog.

Can I pull it off?

Alice is in a good mood. I can tell by the way she

smiles at me when I get in the car. She is wearing a navy coat with black pumps and a black handbag. Her ever-present folder is beside her on the seat and her white hair is gleaming in the morning sun.

We're in Grandmaman's Rolls-Royce, and her driver, Officer Heinz-Walther Werther is behind the wheel.

As we navigate the narrow winding road out of the palace complex and then through the cobblestone streets of Waldenburg town everything looks exactly as it does every other day of the year. But I don't feel the same. I'm nervous and anxious and hope I'll do a good job – and that no one will stand up and say, "Hey, aren't you Tiara Girl?" Mostly, I try not to think that in less than an hour I'll have to give a speech in front of **A THOUSAND** people!!!

I'm about to relax because Alice hasn't asked me which dress I'm wearing, when suddenly she sees the blue fabric peek out from under my coat.

She looks surprised as she says, "What happened to the pink dress, Princess Lily? I was certain you'd choose it."

"Umm…"

Alice is looking at me, waiting.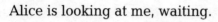

"Umm…well, I was going to wear it and then…"

"Yes?" She is pursing her lips, which is not a good sign.

"I thought it might bring me good luck to match the blue sky. And then Mum and Grandmaman gave me this butterfly brooch this morning," I say as I point to it. "And because the pink dress is more embellished than this one I thought that with the brooch it might all be a bit too much…you know?" I look at Alice and try to smile a normal smile.

Alice is very quiet for a moment. And then she says, "You are full of surprises, Princess Lily. Yesterday I saw you looking most…*un-princess-like* in that bright green wig and glittery outfit and today you are dressed like a perfect princess… Perhaps there are two of you?"

For one terrifying moment I think Alice has figured out my secret, but suddenly she smiles and I realize she is joking.

I shrug my shoulders and do my best to keep my

voice relaxed – when inside I'm **SO NOT RELAXED**.

"Well, you know, Alice, Grandmaman once told me that when I'm at the palace I should dress as I like, but when I'm carrying out my royal duties I should dress in a more classic style...so I guess I'm just following her advice – and yours." I hold my breath as Alice watches me.

"Hmm...yes, I see," she finally says. "Well, you look lovely, Lily. And I'm happy to hear that our advice doesn't just go in one ear and out the other."

As Werther turns the car out of town and onto the road that will take us up the mountainside to the village of Tannenspitz and the animal rescue centre I can't help but wonder if I'm the first princess in my family to have so much to worry about on her first day of royal duty? Has any other Waldenburg Crown Princess had to pretend to be such a perfect princess? Or worry about her secret online persona being exposed?

I royally doubt it!!!

Everything looks so peaceful as we drive on and I start to think this morning will be more easy-peasy than I'd imagined. Then we round the last big bend in the road before the village and my mouth drops open. Police are patrolling the barriers that have been put up to keep the crowds off the road. There are hundreds and hundreds of people lining the way, smiling and waving Waldenburg flags. Werther slows the car and we gently roll towards the top of the high street.

"It's time to start waving, Princess Lilian," Alice reminds me.

I do as she says all the way up to where the mayor and a few other town dignitaries are waiting for me.

I've never been in these kinds of crowds **ON MY OWN** before…but today all of these people are here to see **ME**.

"Are you ready?" Alice asks.

I start to relax as I look more closely at the faces watching me through the windows. Everyone looks so happy and excited.

"Yes, Alice," I say, "I'm ready."

Alice nods at Werther's reflection in the rear-view mirror and he smiles as he jumps out of the car to open my door. I step onto the pavement and hear a cheer as I walk towards the mayor and shake her hand.

HOLY ROYAL MACARONI!!!!!

My first day of royal duty has started!

The morning passes in a blur of action, waving and smiling.

Alice followed me on my walkabout. It was actually fun because everyone was so friendly and excited. It turns out that the crowd was larger than expected – over two thousand Waldenburgers showed up. Alice was so busy and pleased at how well the morning was going that she mentioned nothing more about my dress choice.

There was one moment, though, when I totally thought my cover had been blown.

I was leaning over the barrier to speak with a girl about my age. She was holding a poster with a photo of me on it – the photo from the palace Instagram – and a flower posy for me, too. She asked if she could have a selfie with me and when I leaned in to explain to her that it's against the Royal Rules, she said that I reminded her of her favourite vlogger, Tiara Girl. Alice came to stand beside us at just that moment, to take the posy from my hand, and I wanted to disappear into the pavement.

"Somehow you and Tiara Girl look similar. I mean, I have no idea what Tiara Girl *really* looks because she keeps her identity a secret…but when I saw this photo on the palace Instagram I thought, *Wow, you look like style sisters…*" I watched as Alice looked up at the poster and then back to me, her lips pursed. I was wondering how I could get myself out of this when suddenly the girl said, "But when I see you in person you look absolutely nothing like Tiara Girl. Her style is so colourful – but you look like the perfect princess!" I sighed with relief and out of the corner of my eye I saw Alice move on.

PHEW!

I was given lots of flower posies by a group of girls from a local kindergarten – all of whom were wearing plastic tiaras. I would have loved to share some of my Tiara Girl customizing tips with them but one look at

Alice was enough to remind me not to. (**FYI**: in my family it is a tradition that we collect every flower posy that we are given during walkabouts and then donate them to various hospitals and care homes when the day is over.)

The photo opportunities went well enough – although I think it's a really uncomfortable feeling to stand, frozen in place, for minutes on end, smiling, while journalists click away with their cameras. After about ten seconds it starts to feel fake – and I guess it is, actually, but what can I do? Alice says that posing and looking like I enjoy it is part of being royal and that I'll get better at it with time.

I'm not so sure…

Lilian, my namesake foal, is gorgeous, though. Photos were taken of me feeding her carrots and my smiles were totally **NOT** fake. She also seemed to like my butterfly brooch because she nibbled it with her soft velvety lips. I whispered to her that I'd make her a tiara one day – as long as I could be sure that it remained a secret between her and me.

Everyone was really kind and the morning had such a buzz about it. I loved the new centre and although it is a very sad thing to be an animal without a forever home, at least the Hairy Hounds and Happy Horses Animal Rescue Centre is a happy place to live until you are adopted. I told the Ingolds I'd keep in touch because they are an amazing team and I think they do really special work with every animal they take in.

When we were driving back to the palace Alice surprised me by saying, "Princess Lily, today went splendidly. You had a kind word for everyone, you were patient and your speech was flawless – you spoke slowly and clearly. And because you'd memorized your speech, I also noticed how much eye contact you were able to make while speaking. *That* went down very well with the audience. Also, you made some very insightful comments to the mayor about the rescue centre, so I knew you had studied your notes. Well done!"

I smiled and thanked Alice, although on the inside I was dying to jump up and down and call Leonie to tell her that our plan had royally worked!

 Chapter FOURTEEN

2.01 p.m., at school

"Mission accomplished: I saw you on the news and you really looked like the perfect princess!!!" Leonie whispers to me excitedly as she adds more dots to her mother's face – we're still working on our pointillism project. "There was no way anyone could have confused you with Tiara Girl!"

"For a moment, though, I was sure my cover was blown when a girl in the crowd started talking to me about how I could be style sisters with Tiara Girl and Alice was standing right there! But luckily the girl then said that I looked like such a perfect princess that I couldn't possibly be Tiara Girl."

Leonie and I high-five each other because our **Perfect Princess Plan** has worked! **YAY!!!** Monsieur Falck looks at us and says that high-fiving is not a part of pointillism technique.

"So it seems that all has ended well – at least for now…"

I nod as I add my signature at the bottom of Cupcake's portrait.

As Leonie and I walk to our lockers I see Max coming towards me. It looks like his nose is back to normal, although he turns bright red as he approaches. For once he doesn't stop to talk to me about gender equality but instead says he'll see me at Waltz Class and moves briskly along, as if he's worried he might end up with another ice pack on his face if he spends any more time with me. Ha ha! I guess that was one good thing about my first waltz lesson!

My phone suddenly buzzes.

Hi Tiara Girl! And welcome to your channel!

You have one new direct message

Dear Tiara Girl,

We are a company called Pony Pizzazz and we produce pony and rider accessories. We have become fans of your vlog and love the clothes you make for yourself and the accessories you make for your animals – in particular, for your pony.

In fact, we are so impressed with your DIY style that we'd love to work with you! If you think you'd be interested in designing a collection of matching rider and pony accessories for us, please get in touch. We hope to hear from you soon!

With our best wishes,

The team at Pony Pizzazz

WHAT?!?!??! OMG!!!!!

I've been asked to design a collection of matching pony and rider accessories!!! For Pony Pizzazz! I know the company because Cupcake has some of their accessories! They make **THE** cutest things.

This has been **THE BEST** day of my life!

Even if I did have to start my royal duties!

I show Leonie the message and watch her while she reads it. She looks just as surprised as I was.

"**OMG!!!**" she says. "You're going to be a real fashion designer!!!"

"**YESSSSSS!!!!**"

She gives me a knowing stare. "You know what that means?"

I shake my head.

"Now that you're a vlogger and designer, you really have to stick to our **Perfect Princess Plan!**"

"I will," I say – even though the thought of wearing perfect princess dresses for the rest of my life gives me the royal zzzzs. **BUT WHAT CHOICE DO I HAVE IF I'M GOING TO BE A DESIGNER?!?!?!**

Anyway, when I think about it, this morning's Crown Princess stuff was actually kind of...*fun*. Like, yes, I was nervous about making my speech and also I was worried about being found out as Tiara Girl. But in the end everything went well. I managed to pull my speech off without a hitch in front of **TWO THOUSAND** people, I met many kind and wonderful Waldenburgers, and opening the rescue centre made a lot of people happy – not to mention some very special animals.

And in a weird kind of way it sort of felt as if it was something I was meant to do... I mean, I know I'm always complaining about Princess Class and the Royal Rules and everything, but at the same time, today I realized that I also want to do all the queen-to-be stuff well because Waldenburg is a special place – and it continues to be special because of Mum and Grandmaman and all my queenly ancestors before them and I can't let them and Waldenburgers down, can I?

At the same time being creative and sharing my fashion DIY ideas on my vlog also feels like it's something I'm meant to do.

Can a person spend their life doing two such different things? Maybe one day I'll be able to do both without keeping the vlog a secret?

"What are you thinking about?" Leonie suddenly asks.

"The future."

"And...?"

"And I think it's going to be **ROYALLY AWESOME!**"

HOW I STARTED MY TIARA GIRL VLOG:

1. ## MY VLOG NEEDED TO STAND OUT!

   There are masses of teen lifestyle and fashion vlogs out there, but what I think makes mine different is that I always include a tiara. I sometimes wear a plastic glitter one that I won at the Waldenburg Summer Fair last year. Zoë always has one on and Coco sometimes does too. I think it's fun, plus everyone knows that my vlog is called Tiara Girl for a reason.

2. ## I VLOG ABOUT WHAT I LOVE! I wanted

   to vlog about something I'm passionate about and something that made me smile. For my first video Cupcake and I wore matching glitter make-up and hairstyles. It may sound weird but, honestly, it looked super cute.

3. **I TRY TO POST REGULARLY!** This can be tricky because as you can see it's very hard for me to be alone, or I have a ton of homework, or Princess Class, and so no time to film a video. But to keep my followers excited about what I'm doing, I have to post regularly.

4. **SHORTER IS BETTER!** I don't want my audience to be bored, so I try to keep things snappy or I know everyone will get the zzzzs. I think two snappy minutes are better than five zzzz-y ones.

5. **STAYING SAFE!** Leonie made sure to tell me to stay safe online. So, like other vloggers, I never talk about where I live, or my school, or any details that people can identify me by. I know how important that is because my vlog can be viewed by anyone, anywhere (plus the palace mustn't know). And I **LOVE LOVE LOVE** being Tiara Girl!

SIX DIFFERENCES BETWEEN LIVING IN A PALACE AND LIVING IN A HOUSE:

People always want to know what it's like to live in a palace but because I've always lived in one I'm not sure how to answer. I mean, even if it has lots of towers and hundreds of rooms and is set on the top of a high mountain, it's still my **HOME**.

Then again, my **BFF**, Leonie, says that living in a palace is **WAY** different than living in a normal house…

1. **FOOTSTEPS.** Yes, footsteps. Here's what I mean…if you're ever asked to sleepover at a palace try the following: at night make sure your bedroom window is open, then get into bed, turn out the lights and listen; soon you'll hear footsteps quietly padding around outside. At first you might think it's someone trying to break into the palace, or even a ghost, but it isn't – it's soldiers. They walk all around the

palace day and night, rain or shine, guarding. It took Leonie some time to get used to this because she says that at a normal house, if you hear footsteps outside your bedroom window in the middle of the night, it's definitely a burglar.

2. **THE CLOCKS.** At Leonie's house her family look at their phones to see what time it is – although I know Mrs Leonberger keeps a very loud alarm clock on her bedside table. But palaces tend to have large, gold clocks ticking in almost every room. Plus, most palaces also have a clock tower that chimes loudly on the hour, all day and night, so everyone at the palace always knows what time it is.

3. **THE SILENCE.** Leonie says that in most houses you know what everyone is doing because you can hear them – and I know it's true from the times I've visited her. Sometimes, at Leonie's house, I can even hear Mr Leonberger gargling with his mouthwash in the mornings.

And I can tell when Mrs and Mr

Leonberger are in the kitchen cooking because I hear the saucepans and dishes clattering even if I'm upstairs in Leonie's bedroom. That never happens at home because the kitchen is a twenty minute walk away from my bedroom! So apart from the ticking clocks, all I hear is silence.

4. **THE SPACE.** I know that might seem obvious, but what I mean is that while Leonie says that most people know every room in their house, if you live in an eight-hundred room palace you probably haven't been into every room. A palace usually has so many rooms that there are even forgotten or abandoned ones – like my secret turret!

5. **BALLROOMS.** Every palace has a ballroom! That's because queens and kings throughout history have been expected to entertain on a lavish scale. Our ballroom is two storeys high and has mirrors all along one wall and large windows on the opposite side. Two rows of huge

crystal chandeliers hang from the ceilings. I love our ballroom – even if I have my Waltz Lessons in it!

6. **HOUSE-TRAINING YOUR PUPPY!** I bet I've surprised you with this one, but trust me – if you live in a palace it can take forever just to take your puppy outside. At Leonie's house there is a door straight into the garden from the living room – **SO** easy-peasy. I on the other hand, might have to go through about thirty rooms and down two or three different staircases before I reach the nearest door to the palace gardens. Good thing Coco was such a royally well-behaved puppy!

MY FOUR TOP TIPS FOR CHANNELLING YOUR SPEECH-MAKING INNER QUEEN:

Like Alice always says: "A princess can't just wear tiaras and wave from balconies – she also has to do her duty." And that means doing queen-to-be stuff, like giving speeches.

1. **MEMORIZE YOUR SPEECH!** I know – **NOT** fun. But the better memorized your speech is, the more eye contact you'll be able to give your audience. You'll also sound more natural if you don't have to read from your notes.

2. **RELAX AND SPEAK SLOWLY!** Before you give your speech make sure to practise out loud, preferably in front of your **BFF** or parents, so that you get a feel for the right tempo.

3. Whether you will be using a microphone or not, be sure to speak loudly enough. Grandmaman says I won't be able to inspire

Waldenburgers if I sound like a small mountain mouse and I guess she has a point.

4. Before you go on stage it might help to quietly remember a moment when you did something really well, like that afternoon when you played football better than ever or received high marks on a school paper. Walk on stage feeling confident, and knowing that **YOU ARE ROYALLY AWESOME!!!**

ROYAL RULES ON WHAT TO WEAR ON DIFFERENT OCCASIONS:

Being a princess means lots of Royal Rules on what to wear. Sometimes they're **SO** not fun, but sometimes dressing up for different occasions can be pretty fabulous! Here's what I would wear to...

* **TEA WITH A QUEEN:** My mum is a queen so (Royal Confession): I don't always dress up to have tea with her. **BUT**...if I was invited to have tea with the Queen of the United Kingdom, for instance, I know Alice would say I should wear a dress, tights and some cute ballerinas. Also, Grandmaman would insist that my hair be tidy and my hands clean. And I would never lift my little finger into the air when I hold my teacup. I know that's what you see in the movies – but no real life princess would ever do that!

* **A BALL:** Balls at a palace normally have a formal dress code (Royal **FYI**: a "dress code" is a bunch of rules that tells you what to wear) so

that means only one thing: ballgown and tiara. **SO EXCITING!** A ballgown should be long, and I'd usually have a matching shawl or little cape, in case I step out in the garden for some fresh air. But Grandmaman's favourite Royal Rule is: no matter how much your tiara sparkles, **YOU** should shine even more – with good manners and a big smile!

* **GO RIDING:** Grandmaman taught me when I was very young that **ANY TIME** I am outside (riding or walking or shopping) I'm fair game for paparazzi photographers. Often they'll be hiding, so even if I'm riding Cupcake deep in the forest I have to remind myself that someone could be taking my picture. That means I have to ask myself before I leave the palace: would I like to see myself on the cover of a magazine looking like I do now? To ride I always dress in riding breeches and a matching polo shirt and fleece jacket. My hair is usually in a plait or pony-tail (under my safety helmet).

* **CUT A RIBBON**: I really have to follow the Royal Rules for this one because **ALL EYES** can be on me. That means a dress that won't easily wrinkle, shoes that are pretty but comfortable (in case I have to do a long walkabout) and, maybe – if the occasion is a fancy one – a matching hat. If the day is windy or cold I have a matching coat, too. Oh, and a small handbag (just big enough for my phone – which must be turned **OFF** during all royal duties – and a lip gloss) to hang over my wrist or across my body. My hands must be free so that I can shake hands and hold flowers and wave.

Royally yours, **Lily** xoxo